"You need to teach me."

"Pardon me?" Olivia Mae asked.

"You need to give me dating lessons," Noah said.

"What do you mean?"

"You and me. We'll go on a few dates…three. That would be a *gut* number. You can learn how to do most things if you do it three times."

"That's a ridiculous suggestion."

"Why? I learn better from doing."

"Do you?"

"I've already learned not to take a girl to a gas station or a picnic, but who knows how many more dating traps are waiting for me to stumble into them."

"So this would be…a learning experience."

"It's a perfect solution." He studied her closely and then reached forward and tugged on her *kapp* string, something no one had done to her since she'd been a young teen in school with a crush on a boy.

"I can tell by the shock on your face and the way you're twirling that *kapp* string that I've made you uncomfortable. It's a *gut* idea, though. We'd keep it businesslike—nothing personal."

Vannetta Chapman has published over one hundred articles in Christian family magazines, receiving over two dozen awards from Romance Writers of America chapter groups. She discovered her love for the Amish while researching her grandfather's birthplace of Albion, Pennsylvania. Her first novel, *A Simple Amish Christmas*, quickly became a bestseller. Chapman lives in the Texas Hill Country with her husband.

Books by Vannetta Chapman

Love Inspired

Indiana Amish Brides

A Widow's Hope
Amish Christmas Memories
A Perfect Amish Match

Visit the Author Profile page at Harlequin.com.

A Perfect
Amish Match

Vannetta Chapman

HARLEQUIN® LOVE INSPIRED®

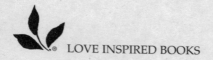

LOVE INSPIRED BOOKS

Recycling programs for this product may not exist in your area.

ISBN-13: 978-1-335-53915-1

A Perfect Amish Match

www.Harlequin.com

Printed in U.S.A.

Many waters cannot quench love,
neither can the floods drown it.
—*Song of Solomon* 8:7

By this shall all men know that
ye are my disciples,
if ye have love one to another.
—*John* 13:35

This book is dedicated to Beth Scott,
a dear friend. God blessed me
when our paths crossed.

Acknowledgments

Continued thanks to my editor,
Melissa Endlich, for guiding me through the
Love Inspired process. All of the people at
Harlequin have been a joy to work with.
A special thanks to my agent, Steve Laube,
for his wisdom, hard work and sense of humor.

I wouldn't even attempt to write without the
help of my family, pre-readers and friends.
You all are a constant source of inspiration.

And finally, "Giving thanks always for all things
unto God and the Father in the name of our
Lord Jesus Christ" (*Ephesians* 5:20).

Chapter One

Olivia Mae Miller had her hands covered in flour and was breading chicken breasts to slip into the oven when *Mammi* called out, "Someone's at the door."

It was late Wednesday afternoon, the first day of May. She'd opened the doors and windows to allow the spring breeze into the house. She could just make out the silhouette of a tall man through the screen door. Olivia Mae added dashes of salt, pepper and garlic to the chicken, then popped the baking dish into the oven. Finally she snagged a dish towel off the counter and hurried through the living room, hoping the sight of a stranger wouldn't upset her grandfather. Some days he could become quite agitated. Other days he was sure the person was a long-lost relative.

"Can I help you?" She peered through the

screen, looking up to take the measure of the man on their porch.

"Are you Olivia Mae?"

"Ya." Still she didn't step outside. Maybe he would go away if she wasn't overly friendly. She had dinner to finish preparing—potatoes and corn and salad. The doctors said small amounts of salad were very important for people her grandparents' age. She really couldn't afford to run behind on their schedule. Evenings were difficult when they didn't manage to tuck *Daddi* into bed early. She almost said, "We're not interested," to shoo away the man.

But then the stranger held up a wooden box that had been tucked under his arm. "I believe this is yours."

"Oh, my." Still wiping flour off her hands, she pushed through the door, forcing him to take a few steps back. "Where did you find that?"

He placed the box in her hands. "I'm an auctioneer over in Shipshewana, and it was in a lot—"

"From my grandparents' old house. I must have left it there, and then they moved. But I still don't understand how you ended up with it."

"I thought it was something that my *mamm* would like."

She must have looked alarmed, because he quickly added, "I didn't actually buy it. I couldn't. Since I'm the auctioneer, that wouldn't be proper. I asked my *bruder* to bid on it, which he did."

The man was rambling and refused to make eye contact. He seemed nervous for some reason. Olivia Mae pulled her gaze from him to study the box she was holding—cherry wood, sanded smooth, with a trio of butterflies carved in the bottom right-hand corner.

"After the auction, when I opened it, I saw the papers that had your name on them."

Her head jerked up at the mention of her letters. "They're still in here?"

"I didn't—didn't read them. Just saw your name, and my youngest *bruder* was standing there, and he knew you—knew of you. We both agreed it should be returned to the rightful owner. Didn't seem likely that you would intentionally auction it with the letters inside."

She moved over to one of the porch rockers, and Tall-Dark-and-Handsome followed her. Olivia Mae sank into the chair, opened the box and unfolded the top sheet. It was her handwriting all right, from so many years ago. Pain as sharp as any paring knife sliced through her heart. She shook her head, refolded the letter, gently closed the lid and turned her attention to her visitor.

"It would seem I owe you then."

"Of course not. We have a process for things

like that—when something is auctioned but shouldn't be."

"So your *bruder* was refunded his money?"

"He was."

"What's your name?"

"Noah. Noah Graber." Instead of looking at her as he spoke, he stared out over the porch railing at her pitiful herd of sheep in the adjacent pasture—if you could call six a herd.

"And you live here in Goshen?"

"I do now. Just moved back." He didn't offer any further explanation about that, but he did add, "My youngest *bruder*, the one who was helping me, is Samuel."

"I know Samuel, as well as Justin."

"Seems everyone knows everyone around here."

"Justin Graber and Sarah Kauffmann. They were married last fall."

Dawning washed across Noah's face.

It was almost comical.

"You're the matchmaker?" He was still standing, and now he glanced at her before looking at his hands, the porch floor, even his horse and buggy. "I recognized your name, but I didn't remember…that you, well, put Justin and Sarah together."

Olivia Mae waved away that thought. "It was

obvious that those two were a perfect match for each other."

"Wasn't obvious to Justin or Sarah. They'd known each other all their lives and never even thought of courting, to hear him tell it."

She'd dropped her gaze to the box and was again focused on it. To see it after all these years, it made her feel young again, made her feel seventeen. But it also reminded her of the painful times that came during and after that year. The deaths of her parents, moving to live with her brothers and then the problems with her grandparents. She could have never imagined then how her *mammi* and *daddi* would come to depend on her, and how inadequately prepared she was for the changes in their health. If she didn't find a way to stem their drastic decline, she knew it would mean a move, and she was convinced that would be the worst possible thing for them.

"I missed the wedding," Noah continued. "I was living in Pennsylvania at the time. Seems I've missed a lot of things around here, but to meet an Amish matchmaker... Well, I wouldn't have ever guessed that, and I wouldn't have thought she'd look like you."

There was something in Noah Graber's voice that pulled her attention away from the wooden box and to his eyes, which were a warm dark brown, like the best kind of chocolate.

"What's that supposed to mean?"

"What's *what* supposed to mean?"

"What am I supposed to look like?"

"Well—"

"Old, maybe. Using a cane. Peering at you over my glasses and shaking my knitting needle at you." She'd come across the stereotype before. She should be used to it by now. "Yes, I'm a matchmaker. Is that something you're interested in?"

"Me? *Nein.*" He shifted uncomfortably on his feet and jerked the straw hat off his head. She wasn't surprised to see that his brown hair curled at the collar. Over six feet, tall as a reed and brown curly hair to boot? Noah Graber could be a cover model for an Amish romance book. As she waited for him to explain why he wasn't interested in dating, a blush crept up his neck. He was easily embarrassed, too? He'd be perfect for Jane, or possibly Francine.

"I wouldn't think that you would need a matchmaker. No doubt you have women following you around at the auction." She motioned toward the other rocker.

He shrugged and perched on the edge of the seat. "Actually I'm single—happily single."

"Is that so?"

"It is."

"And why would that be?"

"Can't see as that's your business."

Olivia Mae laughed. "Fair enough. It's true that I enjoy setting up dates for those who haven't found the love of their life."

Noah shook his head in disbelief. "You believe in that?"

"*Ya.* Don't you?"

"Never really thought about it."

She doubted that was true, but she didn't call him on it. Instead she returned her attention to the box. Running her fingertips across the top, she marveled at the way just holding it took her back to a simpler time, an easier time.

"My *daddi* made it for me. He was quite good with small wood projects, when he was younger. Now…" She pulled in a deep breath. "He gave it to me when I came to visit one summer. I left it at their home, thinking I would be back the next year. But they moved and things…changed."

"I'm surprised it ended up at auction."

How could she explain what *Mammi* and *Daddi* had been through the last few years? She couldn't, and why would she try? This stranger wasn't interested in the particular burdens of their life, so instead she changed the subject.

"I don't remember seeing you at church."

"We didn't meet this past week, and I only moved back the Wednesday before that."

"And already working at the auction house?"

"*Ya*. It's the reason I moved here. They needed another auctioneer so I thought I'd come back home."

Olivia Mae searched his eyes for a moment, long enough that he began to squirm again. There was something he wasn't saying, but she had no reason to press him. As he'd pointed out, he wasn't interested in being matched and beyond that she was simply being nosy.

"Welcome to Goshen, then, though it sounds as if you grew up here."

"I did."

"If it's been more than a few years, I expect it's changed a bit since then."

"Yes and no."

A man of few words. Yes, he would match perfectly with Jane Bontrager. She was a real chatterbox, which would balance them out. She was tall, too—not as tall as Noah Graber, but tall enough that he wouldn't feel awkward. Was that why he'd never married? Did he tower over every woman he met?

He pinched the bridge of his nose, as if the entire conversation was painful to him. "Some things always stay the same—especially in Amish communities."

"Yes. I suppose so." She smiled, stood and said, "*Danki* very much for bringing this out to me."

Noah seemed to realize he was being dismissed. He nodded once and headed down the porch steps when there was a clatter of dishes inside the house.

Olivia Mae was already moving toward the door.

A woman shouted, and then a man hollered something in return.

"Do you need help?"

"*Nein*. We're fine." Which was categorically not true, but she wasn't about to reveal as much to a man she barely knew, and one that probably wouldn't last in town long enough to see the summer flowers.

She hurried inside, allowing the screen door to bang shut behind her. Matchmaking was good and fine, but it was what she did to relax. Her priority was the two dear old people who now looked up at her in surprise—as if she'd popped in from thin air.

"I've got that, *Mammi*."

"Turned my back on him for one minute..." *Mammi* had a dish towel and was attempting to clean up the coffee that had spilled on his shirt. The mug sat on the floor next to *Daddi*'s chair.

Olivia Mae went for the broom and dustpan.

She returned to the sitting room and began sweeping up shattered pieces of a small dish on the opposite side of the room, where it had apparently been flung.

Mammi continued to blot at the coffee stains, but *Daddi* was having none of it. He captured her hands in one of his, which were still strong—they were the same hands that had felled trees and planted fields and carved Olivia Mae's letter box. "Don't bother me with that, Rachel. Did you see the size of that hog? Nearly knocked over my chair trying to get at your peanut-butter squares."

Olivia Mae and *Mammi* shared a look, but neither corrected him. They'd learned long ago that doing so only made matters worse.

Noah spent most of the drive home wondering if he should have gone back up the porch steps to make sure everyone was all right. As he'd walked away, he had distinctly heard an old man's shouting. Olivia Mae had clearly not wanted help—she'd practically slammed the screen door shut without a single look back.

His mood jostled between concern for this woman he didn't know, aggravation at his brother and curiosity over what was in the box. She had barely glanced at the top sheet, though plainly she'd recognized it instantly.

Noah was twenty-nine years old, and it wasn't lost on him that all the fine women—women like Olivia Mae Miller—were taken. No doubt her husband had been out in the fields or in the barn with the animals, though he had wondered at the absence of children. Most Amish households had a whole passel.

She had struck him as quintessentially Amish. Thick brown hair pulled back under her *kapp*, with just enough showing that he'd been sure to notice how it was shot through with blond. Simple Amish frock covered with a clean apron. Brown eyes that seemed to be both laughing and taking in everything at the same time. She reminded him of a teacher he'd had his last year of school—she'd been young and seemed impossibly beautiful and even then he couldn't understand why she was teaching.

That was it. She'd reminded him of a teacher, and he'd felt like a schoolboy squirming under her gaze.

Teacher! Ha. Perhaps she read romance books when she wasn't tending to her children. That would explain her fascination with true love. He'd nearly laughed at her, but stopped when he saw the serious look on her face. She was a believer—no doubt about that. Why shouldn't she be? For Olivia Mae life had turned out the way it was supposed to. For him? Not so much.

His mind threatened to turn toward his past failed relationships, but he shook his head and focused on the scene in front of him instead.

He pulled into his parents' farm, which was one of the larger properties in Goshen. It wasn't that they were wealthy, but with seven boys, his *dat* had made it a priority to purchase any adjacent property as it became available. The result was that they owned close to three hundred acres, which was enough for four farms. Three of his brothers had built adjacent homes, two had moved to nearby counties and one had taken over the family place.

As for Noah, he had no intention of being a farmer.

He'd found his passion, and it was in the auction house.

He directed the buggy horse into the barn and jumped down from the seat as his two younger brothers emerged from the back stalls.

"Managed to miss most of the work," Samuel said, a smile playing across his lips. Samuel was the youngest of the boys. He'd inherited their *mamm*'s blond hair as well as her shape—short and stocky.

Justin was also short, though thin like Noah. He leaned against a bale of hay as Noah removed the harness from the buggy mare.

"How was Olivia Mae?"

"You sent me to a matchmaker? Really?"

Justin held up his hands in innocence, and Samuel began to laugh. "Can't blame us for trying."

"A matchmaker?"

"You're the one who wanted to return the box. You could have left it at the office, and they would have mailed it to her."

"I thought I was doing the neighborly thing. Instead I walked into a trap."

"A trap?"

"*Mamm* probably put you up to it."

"Now you're being paranoid. *Mamm* didn't even know about the box."

"I'm surprised our community tolerates such."

"Are you kidding? Olivia Mae has been a real asset around here. No fewer than six marriages in the last year are a direct result of her—"

"Meddling?"

"Encouragement."

"Well, I'm not interested."

"Told you that's what he'd say." Samuel nudged Justin and held out his hand. "Pay up."

Grudgingly Justin pulled out his wallet and slipped a five-dollar bill into his brother's hand.

"Seriously? You're betting on my social life?"

Samuel laughed again as he pocketed the money, walked out of the barn and headed across the field toward his own family. Noah finished unharnessing the mare and set her out to pasture as Justin watched.

"Actually we're betting on the absence of your social life," he finally said. "Which isn't quite the same thing."

"So you admit that's why you sent me over there?"

"No. Not at first. Samuel didn't know when you asked him to bid on the box that it was Olivia Mae's."

"This wasn't a setup from the get-go?"

"We don't have the time or energy to be that manipulative. I was standing in the back watching—it being your first auction and all. You did well, by the way."

Noah rolled his eyes and tried not to be distracted by the praise.

"When we realized who the box belonged to, we figured it couldn't hurt for you to meet her."

"So it was more of a coincidence than a setup."

"We just saw it as an opportunity."

Noah grunted.

"But it couldn't hurt to talk to the woman."

"I did. She thanked me for the box, pried into my recent history, and then had to go because of some emergency in the house."

Justin took off his hat and scratched the top of his head. "You know *Mamm* and *Dat* worry."

"Because I'm not married?"

"Because you're not the least bit interested in getting married."

"Why should they worry about that?"

"They don't want you to be alone in your old age."

"I have the six of you, plus your wives and children to keep me company. Not to mention *Mamm* and *Dat* are in excellent health."

"It's not the same as having your own family."

"Says who? You? You've been married what...six months?"

"Never been happier."

"And I'm glad for you."

Justin let that comment slide, but as they walked out of the barn and toward the house he said, "You sound kind of crabby."

"Do I?"

"Maybe she got under your skin."

"Maybe you should mind your own business." The words came out crankier than he'd intended. Noah softened them by shoving his *bruder* and taking off toward the house. And suddenly it was like they were ten years old again and racing for the first hot biscuit.

They tumbled into the house, both laughing, and Noah wondered why his knee had begun to twinge after a short sprint. He was trying to rub it inconspicuously when he glanced up and saw Sarah walk into Justin's arms. He kissed her once and touched her stomach, then they both laughed. They might have only married six months ago, but they'd wasted no time in starting a family.

Noah was honest enough to admit the twinge of envy he felt. It was normal he supposed, not that it changed anything. Olivia Mae might believe in true love. His *bruders* might think he'd be better off married, and his parents might think of him as the last baby to be pushed from the nest, but Noah didn't see it that way.

He planned to establish himself as a good auctioneer.

Maybe he'd buy a small farm after that, something with a barn and a horse pasture—there was certainly no need for fields to cultivate.

He'd settle down all right, but on his own terms.

He understood what his future held, what kind of man he was. He'd be a dependable brother, an excellent uncle, even a good son. He had it in him to be a successful auctioneer. But a husband? *Nein*. That wasn't in his future, and he had the dating history to prove it. Something he didn't plan to share with Olivia Mae.

Chapter Two

Sunday morning dawned cloudy but warm. It seemed to Olivia Mae that *Daddi*'s moods reflected the changing weather. As a farmer, rain had always been a good thing—a sign of God's blessing. *Daddi* sat at the kitchen table, a smile on his face, shoveling scrambled eggs into his mouth as if they were the best thing he'd ever tasted.

"Maybe I'll have a chance to meet that nice young man who visited the other day." *Mammi* refilled their coffee mugs and sat down across from Olivia Mae.

"Nice young man?"

"You know very well who I mean."

"We have a new postman."

"*Nein*. Young *Amish* man."

"Our neighbors dropped by with their new baby."

"Olivia Mae, you know *gut* and well who I

mean, though you've avoided talking about him all week." *Mammi* pointed a fork at Olivia Mae as if in warning, but there was a smile on her face.

"Hmmm. Oh, you mean Noah Graber?"

"Indeed. He seemed like a fine young man."

"How could you tell? You didn't meet him."

"Because you didn't invite him in."

"He was just returning something he'd found. There was no need to invite him in, plus I think he was in a hurry."

"Well, he won't be in a hurry today, and I have a mind to speak with him."

"Oh, please don't do that." Olivia Mae fumbled around for a reason. In truth she simply didn't want her grandmother to attempt setting up a date for her again. The last one had been a disaster. The man had been nearly fifty. She certainly didn't get her matchmaking skills from her grandmother. Thank goodness! In desperation she added, "He's rather the shy sort. I was thinking of maybe setting up something between him and Jane Bontrager."

"Why are you always matchmaking other folks together, but no one seems to catch your interest?"

Olivia Mae wasn't too surprised at the question. It was something *Mammi* tossed at her at least once a week.

"I have my hands full with you and *Daddi*. I have a family of my own. I don't need another."

"Pshaw." *Mammi* plucked a hot biscuit from the basket and broke it open with trembling fingers. The steam rose, and she inhaled deeply before adding a pat of butter. "You know what the Good Book says about taking a log out of your own eye before you worry about your *bruder*'s."

"My *bruders* are doing just fine, but *danki* for your concern."

She thought her grandmother would continue to bat the topic back and forth, but instead, when she looked up, confusion clouded her features. "Elizabeth, I've told you before. It's past time you marry, and I don't think you should put it off. There are plenty of *gut* boys available."

Olivia Mae closed her eyes briefly, said a quick prayer for wisdom and forced a smile. "Yes, *Mammi*. I'll give that some thought."

"And prayer. Don't forget prayer, young lady."

Olivia Mae hopped up to clean the dishes so they could leave for church on time. But as she washed and rinsed, she wasn't thinking about the service, she was thinking about *Mammi* calling her by her mother's name. Olivia Mae didn't even look like her mother—she took after her father. Both of her parents had perished in an accident ten years ago and she missed them as sorely as if it had happened the week before.

Daddi's dementia was a terrible thing to watch, but it was *Mammi*'s slips into the past that frightened her more. She couldn't possibly care for her grandfather and grandmother by herself, not to mention that the house was starting to show signs of neglect. She would ask for help if she needed it. Of course she would, but she knew what her *bruders*' answer would be— they had wanted to move *Mammi* and *Daddi* to Maine years ago.

She couldn't imagine taking them away from what was familiar. As far as the house, she could ask the bishop for help and a work crew would be there the following week, but she hesitated to do that, too. Her church family had already done so much to help when *Daddi* was in the hospital last month. She knew they didn't mind, but she didn't want to be the type of person who only asked for help but never gave.

So she bought old sweaters at garage sales, unraveled and washed the yarn and used it for her knitting. She was able to scatter the shawls and sweaters and blankets throughout their community. That and matchmaking were the only ways she knew to give back.

And she prayed, but not for a beau. That would only complicate things. Who would want to take on a twenty-seven-year-old wife, a small farm, a dwindling herd of sheep that she thought of as pets, and tottering grandparents? It seemed too much to ask, in her opinion. Best that she keep her problems to herself and bury her own dreams. Sometimes life called on you to sacrifice.

Mammi and *Daddi* were definitely worth sacrificing for.

Olivia Mae didn't involve herself in someone else's life unless they asked. But during their church service Sunday morning, she couldn't help watching Noah Graber and Jane Bontrager. They sat as far from each other as possible. Noah was on the men's side of the aisle, closer to the front. Jane was near the back, helping with her nieces. Noah didn't seem aware of Jane at all, which wasn't unusual in Olivia Mae's experience. It was one of the reasons that older men remained bachelors. They weren't even looking for love.

What was it that Noah had said?

I'm single—happily single.

He wouldn't be the first man to think so.

Their opening hymn had ended and the ministers had filed into the barn. The doors were open wide, allowing in the fresh spring air, but rain threatened so they'd opted to have the church service under cover. Now they all stood for the *Oblied*, and for a moment Olivia Mae forgot about Noah and Jane and even her grand-parents. She allowed the words of the praise song to flow over her, to rise from her heart. She felt, in those few moments, transported to a place without difficult days and hard decisions. She felt like the young girl who had written the letters to herself, the letters that were in the box Noah had brought to her.

She'd tried to read them. The evening he'd given her the box, she'd waited until she'd set-tled down for the night and then she'd once again unfolded the top sheet. She'd instantly been transported back to the summer of her seventeenth year, when her dreams were still fresh and hopeful. Each sheet contained a let-ter to herself that she'd penned quite seriously over the course of the summer. Where had she come up with that idea?

But the words she'd written seemed to come from a different person. The naiveté of her thoughts and hopes and dreams was too painful.

So she'd folded the letter back up, and had gently placed the box on top of her dresser, then flung her *kapp* over it so she wouldn't have to stare at it.

She tried to focus on the sermons. The first was something about Joshua and Moses and the lost Israelites. Standing between her grand-mother and her neighbor, Olivia Mae prayed, sang, kneeled and stood. She felt as if she was going through the motions, but the ritual soothed her nonetheless. After all, *Gotte* was in control last week, and he was still in control.

Even though *Daddi*'s condition seemed to be worse…

Even though *Mammi* grew more unpredict-able each day…

Bishop Lucas stood and startled Olivia Mae out of her daydreams. He'd been their bishop for over six months now, but still she was sur-prised that it wasn't Atlee who offered their blessing over the meal, who sent them out to be *the people of Gotte*, as he was so fond of saying. She was sure that Lucas would make a fine bishop, though he seemed awfully young at fifty-two. The truth was that in her heart she missed Atlee. He'd been like a wise old *onkel* to her. He'd been someone that she could be com-pletely honest with.

Another hymn, and then they were dismissed and she was hurrying to check on *Daddi*, who insisted he was fine. Several of the men told her not to worry, they would take care of her grandfather.

Mammi was already standing behind the serving line when she joined it. She reached out and touched Olivia Mae's arm, and a flash of understanding passed between them. Being away from the farm was good, but being in public was always nerve-racking. There was just no telling what *Daddi* would do.

Her *mammi*'s look reminded her that they were among friends, among family. She could stop worrying, at least for a few hours.

So Olivia Mae made her way down the line to the table with the main dishes—cold crispy chicken, thick slices of ham, spicy links of sausage. First the elders came through, then the women with the little ones, followed closely by the men. Finally the *youngies*, who filled their plates high, never worrying about calories or fat content. The last group was what Olivia Mae thought of as her people—Amish men and women in their twenties, some recently married and without children, some courting and some who seemed caught in that in-between place.

Jane stepped up with Francine. The two girls were barely twenty and stuck together like peanut butter and honey, which sometimes complicated her matchmaking efforts.

"*Gudemariye*, Olivia Mae." Jane smiled at her brightly—expectantly.

"And to you."

Francine leaned forward. "We heard you were setting up a match for Noah Graber."

"*Nein*. Noah's not interested." Olivia Mae pushed a plate of sandwiches forward, trying to buy herself some time. "I would like to talk to you, though, if you have a minute."

"We'll save you a place." Their heads together and giggling, both Jane and Francine moved toward the dessert table.

She'd thought nearly everyone was through the line the first time, and was looking to make sure that *Mammi* had made herself a plate, when Noah stepped in front of her table.

"I heard the fried chicken is *gut* today."

"Did you, now?"

His hat was pushed back on his head, once again revealing the curly hair, and he was actually making eye contact with her. No doubt he felt safer with the table between them—she wasn't going to jump over it and drag him toward a woman he might feel pressured to court. She couldn't help noticing he was in a better mood, as well. Perhaps because he wasn't on her front porch. Men like Noah relaxed on what they thought of as neutral ground. She'd have to suggest he take Jane to a restaurant in town. A family dinner would be too much pressure.

"Too bad there's not any chicken left."

"I gather you'd like some."

"It's why I'm standing here with no meat on

my plate—my *bruders* insisted that I had to try it."

"Smart guys, your *bruders*." Olivia Mae opened the cooler under the table, pulled out her large Tupperware container and scooted it toward him. "I always make extra."

The grin he gave her caused butterflies to twirl in her stomach. Yes, this one could be a charmer. She only needed someone who was willing to push past his disinterested facade, smooth the rough edges and convince him that he wasn't *happily single*.

He thanked her for the chicken and moved toward the dessert table. Tall and handsome. There was no way she was letting Noah Graber get away from their community. His family was here. He belonged here! He probably faced a contented future with a house full of children.

No woman can be happy with fewer than seven to cook for.

The old proverb danced through her mind. She didn't completely agree with it. After all, she was happy right now. But then, that was a different story. She didn't abide gender stereotypes, but she did believe that men were happier with families. Hadn't she read an article in the grocery checkout line about that very thing? Something about men living five years longer if they were married, and up to seven if they had children.

When she thought of it in those terms, she wasn't prying her way into Noah's life, she was looking out for his health. Isn't that what the *people of Gotte* were supposed to do?

She plopped a crispy chicken leg onto her plate, added a scoop of macaroni salad and a slice of cheese and chose a chocolate brownie for dessert. She was going to need the calories if she was going to be successful today. They might rest from their daily work on Sundays, but matchmaking was a seven-day-a-week affair.

She made her way to where Jane and Francine were sitting and enjoying their meal.

"Uh-oh. She has that glint in her eye." Francine bumped Jane's shoulder. "And I think it's your turn."

"Why do you say that?"

"Because I had a date two weeks ago, and you haven't had one in… I don't know—a month."

"*Ya.* I'm journaling about my good qualities, like Olivia Mae told me to."

Olivia Mae only raised an eyebrow and bit into her chicken. It really was good. She'd learned the recipe from *Mammi*. The trick was to use a good sprinkling of garlic salt but not too much, and to keep the fire high enough to render the coating crispy but not burnt.

"Just tell us who it is." Francine clasped her hands in her lap and leaned forward. "It is Noah? I bet it is. He's the only new person I see here, and you have a definite new-person glint in your eye."

"I didn't know my eyes were so readable." Olivia Mae wiped at her mouth with her napkin. "Yes, it is Noah, and I think we should give Jane the first try."

"Because I'm taller. That's it. Right?" Jane slumped down in her seat. "Why do I have to be so—"

"Three things."

Jane rolled her eyes.

"I'm serious about this—you both know I am. Our first step toward progress is to defeat those negative thoughts in your mind. Now tell me three positive things about your height."

Francine giggled, but Jane screwed up her face as if she hadn't been presented with this question a dozen times. She had. Olivia Mae thought it was her biggest obstacle to finding a suitable man. Jane wasn't that tall, but in her mind she was an ostrich. It didn't help that her first few dates had been with very short men, which only served to reinforce the gangly image she had of herself.

"I can reach the top shelf in the pantry."

"Gut."

"I've stopped growing."

"Not sure that's a positive thing, but go on."

"It's something I inherited from my *dat*, who I adore. So it's… I don't know—nice to be like him in some way."

Olivia Mae put down her fork, which was filled with macaroni salad. "I think we've had a breakthrough. You genuinely meant that."

"Ya. Maybe the journaling is helping, because it occurred to me that even though I don't enjoy being taller than most men, I love the fact that I have something in common with my *dat*."

"I suspect you have a lot in common with him."

"Back to the dating thing…" Francine was much more invested in the matchmaking process, maybe too much. Her enthusiasm tended to frighten men. It was one of the reasons that Olivia Mae thought that Jane might be a better match for someone as shy as Noah.

"I only met Noah earlier this week."

"Tell us about him." Francine stole a glance over her shoulder at Noah.

He was sitting three tables away with his *bruders* and their wives. Was he the only Graber son who wasn't married? Olivia Mae thought he was, but she'd have to ask around to be sure. That could work in their favor, too.

"He's nice enough. Obviously he's easy on the eyes."

"I'll say." Francine grinned.

Jane blushed, but she was listening intently.

"He's working as an auctioneer in Shipshe."

"Is that why he moved back?" Jane asked.

"*Ya*, and it's *gut* that he knows what he wants to do. He won't be distracted by that question as some men are—"

"I still can't believe that Elijah took a job at the RV factory." Jane shook her head in obvious disbelief. She'd thought Elijah would settle down and work for the town farrier, but it apparently wasn't destined to be. "He told his *schweschder*, who told me, that working around the horses just wasn't challenging enough. What's not challenging about shoeing horses?"

"Let's focus." Olivia Mae picked up her brownie, took a bite and allowed the sugar and chocolate to work their magic. Why was it that things you weren't supposed to eat a lot of were so delicious? "Seems to me that Noah might be self-conscious about his height."

"How tall is he?" Jane asked.

"A little over six feet, I think. I didn't exactly measure him when he came by the house." She hadn't meant to say that. One glance at Jane and Francine told her she'd have to go through the entire story of how he'd returned her box, so she did so quickly. "Anyway. He's back in town, working at the auction house, and he says he's happily single."

"Uh-oh." Jane sat up straighter, which was another improvement. She used to always slump, trying to make herself shorter.

"That's what they all say," Francine reminded them. "His own *bruder*—Justin—told you that he wasn't interested in dating at all. That it was a waste of time! Look at him now. He's happily married and expecting a *boppli*."

"Sometimes that makes things easier, when another person in the family has been successfully matched. Other times…" Olivia Mae noticed Noah was being teased by his *bruders*. He glanced toward her table, shook his head, picked up his plate and walked away. "Other times it can make a man more resistant to change."

"Why am I not encouraged by this entire talk?" Jane began to chew on her thumbnail, but tucked her hands back into her lap when she noticed Olivia Mae watching. "Sounds like he's not interested at all. What's your plan?"

"My plan is to convince him that it's his idea."

Chapter Three

Noah made a point of avoiding Olivia Mae after lunch. His brothers had had a hearty laugh over the fact that he'd thought she was married. How was he to know? What kind of matchmaker couldn't find herself a husband? It would be like owning a buggy shop but no buggy. Regardless, he thought it best to avoid her.

It wasn't so terribly hard.

He played baseball. She sat with the women under the hickory tree.

He had more dessert. She seemed to be avoiding the snack table.

He saw her take two young girls into the sheep pen, then coax one of the new lambs over and show them how to pet the babes so that the mother wouldn't be frightened. He'd almost walked over to her then, just casually, to tease her about being a shepherdess. He'd even remembered a sheep joke that he thought would make her laugh.

But she'd said something to the girls, and they'd hurried out of the pen and toward her grandfather. At least Noah supposed the old guy who was gesticulating wildly was her *daddi*. Olivia Mae and an older woman—her grandmother?—had helped him into the house, and then he hadn't seen her again for a while. He'd almost put the idea behind him—of having a talk with her and setting her straight—when he literally bumped into her coming out of the barn and carrying a large ice cooler.

She juggled the ice cooler, and he plucked it from her hands.

"Leaving so soon?"

"*Ya, Daddi*'s tired."

"I can carry this for you."

She cocked her head and stared up at him.

He squirmed under her inspection. Why did she make him feel like his hat was on backward? "Since I almost ran you over, seems like the right thing to do."

"All right. *Danki*."

They talked about the weather as long as anyone possibly could and then fell into an awkward silence. Her buggy would be the last one in the line. Why had he offered to carry the cooler? It was obviously empty and weighed practically nothing. Fishing around for something to say, he remembered her standing in the sheep pen.

"Where do sheep go on vacation?"

"What?"

"Where do sheep go on vacation?"

"I'm sure I have no idea."

"The Ba-a-aa-hamas."

The look on her face was funnier than the joke.

"Do you do that very often?"

"Do what very often?"

"Tell jokes when you're nervous."

"Who said I was nervous?"

"It's sort of obvious."

They'd reached her buggy. She opened the driver's-side door, fished around inside and pulled out three bungee cords. He strapped the cooler to the back of the buggy, as he tried to think how best to answer her question.

"I'm not nervous exactly. It's only that I wanted to say something to you, and I wasn't sure how to bring up the subject."

"Oh. All right. I'm all ears."

"I'm afraid we started off on the wrong foot."

"How so?"

He knew she knew what he was talking about, but obviously, she wasn't going to make this easier for him. He leaned against her buggy and crossed his arms. "I didn't mean to dismiss what you do. Obviously you provide an important service to our community."

"You mean my knitting?"

"*Nein*. I do not mean your knitting. You know exactly what I'm talking about."

Now she smiled at him—a perky *got-you* smile that had him shaking his head. Was that why she wasn't married? Because she was feisty, with an attitude and a sense of humor? Perhaps she had the idea that she didn't fit into the submissive Amish-woman mold, though his own mother was the same in many ways. Regardless, the fact that Olivia Mae was not married was not his business.

"I'm talking about your matchmaking."

"Oh, that."

"Yes, that."

"You've decided it's an important service?"

"It could be. I see that now."

"*Englischers* have dating sites and apps on their phones," she pointed out.

"I wouldn't know about that."

"Of course you wouldn't."

"I've never even owned a phone."

"Neither have I." She was grinning at him now.

If he didn't know better, he'd think that she

enjoyed baiting him. He forced his eyes away from her adorable face and tried to remember what he'd wanted to tell her.

"Your *bruder* seems happy enough."

"He does. He is, and that's what I mean. You obviously do what you do very well."

"Danki."

"I just wanted to remind you that I'm not on the market."

"Oh, you made that quite clear."

Was she being serious? Or playing with him again? Looking back toward the barn, he saw that more people were leaving. He couldn't keep her here forever. He needed to try a more direct approach.

"I saw you talking to the two girls—the tall one and the heavy one."

"Do you mean Jane and Francine?"

"I guess."

"They're *freinden* of mine. We often talk to each other."

"I'm sure, but as soon as you sat down, and you three put your heads together, the heavier one looked over her shoulder at me."

"Did she, now?"

"You're going to deny it?"

"Deny what?"

"That you were talking to them about setting up a date with me."

"I could set you up with one of them." She tapped her chin and scrunched up her eyes as if she'd never considered such a thing. "But I thought you weren't interested."

Noah laughed out loud. "You are twisting what I'm saying every which way. I'm *not* interested. I told you I wasn't on Wednesday, and I'm still not. I wanted to make sure we're clear about that."

"Crystal."

"Gut."

"Gut."

Another awkward silence followed. She'd caved easier than he'd thought she would. He'd expected her to list the reasons that either girl would be a good match for him. Didn't she think he was dating material? Did she think he was too old or too set in his ways?

He didn't want to talk about that, but he wasn't ready to walk away, either.

"What do you call a sheep that knows karate?"

Olivia Mae rolled her eyes, but a grin was spreading across her face.

"I don't know, Noah. What do you call a sheep that knows karate?"

"A lamb chop."

He walked away then, the sound of her laughter ringing in his ears.

* * *

Unfortunately his good mood didn't last. His father insisted Noah ride up front in the buggy with him on the way home. His mother sat in the back, surrounded by grandchildren. For the first ten minutes, Noah actually enjoyed the ride. Then his *dat* cleared his throat and glanced his direction.

"You know we're glad you're home, son."

"But…"

"No *but*. Your mother and I want you to know that we are grateful to the Lord for bringing you back."

Perhaps he'd misjudged his *dat*'s intent. Maybe he'd anticipated a lecture when there wasn't one headed his way. Noah rested his head against the door and looked out over the Indiana farmland. "I'm glad to be back. Goshen seems…better in some ways. Instead of it feeling like a shoe that's too small, it feels like one that fits just right."

"That's *gut*, but…"

Noah tried to suppress a sigh, without success.

"Just hear me out."

"Of course, *Dat*." It wasn't as if he had a choice. They were still ten minutes from home. It would be childish to ask to be let out and walk, though the thought did cross his mind. Instead he sat up straighter and clasped his hands in front of him.

"I know you enjoy your auction work…"

"It's why I'm here."

"However, I'd like you to leave some time free to learn more about the farm."

"Why would I do that?"

"Because you never learned it as a *youngie*."

"I grew up doing farm chores."

"That's true, but a young man's real training begins about the time that you left—was it when you went to New York or Pennsylvania?" He waved away the question before Noah could answer it. "I want to teach you about farming because every young man needs to know how to plant, grow and harvest a crop."

"*Dat*, I'm not a farmer. I never have been a farmer, and I have no intention of becoming one in the future. I'm an auctioneer."

That statement sat between them as the mare clip-clopped down the road.

Noah could just make out his *mamm* saying something to his nieces, but he couldn't discern her exact words. At least she was preoccupied so that it wasn't two against one, not at this point.

"I appreciate your offer. I do. But times have changed—"

"Every man has to eat and farming is what we do. It's the Amish way."

"Not every Amish man farms. Some are farriers. Others are cabinetmakers."

"And you're an auctioneer."

"A *gut* one, too, if I say so myself."

"It's only that—to me—auctioneering seems like a hobby, not a way to support yourself."

Noah slouched down in his seat. He honestly didn't know how to make his *dat* understand. He didn't know how to explain that there were more opportunities available to Amish folk now. Working in the auction house could provide a good, steady income. It was only that it was different from work that his father's generation had done.

"There's one other thing."

"Of course there is."

"We understand it may seem awkward to date because you're late getting started."

"I dated..."

"And sometimes these things need a little help."

"I thought you were happy to have me at home. Now you're trying to scoot me out of the nest?"

"You're twenty-nine, son."

"I'm aware."

Noah glanced at his *dat*, noticed a furrow of lines between his eyes. He was obviously bound and determined to have his say.

"It's easy at your age to believe that you have an endless number of days in front of you—to plan, to decide, to marry. But that's not true. Every man and woman has a limited amount of time on this earth, and it's our responsibility to put those days to the best use."

"What does this have to do with dating?"

"I'd hate to see you waste the best years of your life."

"Waste them?"

"A family is a *wunderbaar* blessing."

"For most, yes, it is."

"Your *bruder* Justin needed a little help, and your *mamm* and I just want you to know that we see no shame in that."

"Now you're talking about Olivia Mae."

"She's a *gut* woman, and she has a real knack for putting the right people together. I was skeptical at first, too, but seeing the couples she's matched… Well, it's a real gift that she has."

Fortunately their farm had come into view.

Noah's shoulder muscles felt like two giant knots, and a headache was pounding at his temples. How could a twenty-minute ride with his parents make him so tense?

At least he was able to keep his mouth shut for the remainder of the ride. No use telling his father that he had no intention of being matched.

No use pointing out the obvious—that his dating life wasn't anyone's business.

At least his mother hadn't chimed in with her two cents. The last thing he needed was more pressure.

They pulled to a stop in front of the house, the lecture delivered. The evening's chores still waited to be done—even on a Sunday. Horses still had to be fed, cows milked, goats checked. He actually looked forward to the escape of farm work, though it was not what he planned on doing for the rest of his life.

As he was helping the children out of the back seat, his mother stopped beside him, reached up and kissed him on the cheek. "Give it some thought, dear."

He stared after her as she climbed the front porch steps, a grandchild holding on to each hand.

Life was so simple for their generation, with everything laid out in black and white. But Noah had traveled enough to learn two very important things.

He was not, nor would he ever be, a farmer.

And given his dating history, which they knew nothing about, he also wasn't the marrying type.

The only problem would be convincing his family of that.

* * *

It took longer than Olivia Mae thought it would. Exactly ten days later, a familiar buggy pulled down their lane. She was out with the sheep, so instead of hurrying toward the house, she waved her arms over her head, hoping that Noah Graber had come to see her and not her grandparents. He turned the pretty sorrel buggy mare toward her, and pulled up next to the pasture fence. He hopped out and joined her, though she was standing on one side of the fence and he was on the other.

"Where are the rest?"

"Rest of what?"

"Rest of your sheep."

"Oh. This is all we have."

Noah pulled off his hat, held it up to block off the late-afternoon sun and made an exaggerated motion of counting her ewes. "Six?"

"Ya."

"You have six sheep."

"I do, as you've so accurately counted."

"Why couldn't the little lamb play outside?"

Olivia waited, both dreading and looking forward to the punch line.

"It was being ba-a-aaad!" As she shook her head in mock disgust, he plopped the hat back on his head and crossed his arms across the top board of the wooden fence. "I honestly don't know a thing about sheep."

"Though you do know a lot of jokes."

"Tell me about your flock."

She didn't think he was asking for their names, though she had named them all. Instead she simply offered, "They're Lincoln sheep."

"I don't know what that means."

"They're large, as you can see. Ewes can weigh from two hundred to two hundred and fifty pounds."

"I thought they were just fat."

She slapped his arm. "Rams can get up to three hundred and fifty. They're a *gut* sheep to have if you're raising them for their fleece. Lincoln sheep are very long-wooled."

"I can see that."

Olivia Mae laughed. "Wait until you see them just before shearing. This is nothing."

"So you sell their fleece?"

"*Ya*, it's quite popular for spinning and weaving."

"Why do you only have six?"

Olivia Mae shrugged. Though she didn't want to go into it, she understood that making small talk made Noah comfortable, so she played along. "We lost two to predators..."

"Predators?"

"Probably a coyote. That was in January, and

then we had another two that wandered off into the road during a late snowstorm in March. I check the fencing regularly, but they'd somehow found a way through. It was a hard winter."

"I'll say. So you had ten, which doesn't sound like very many, and now you're down to six."

"My initial plan was to slowly build the herd, but…sometimes life doesn't work out like you plan."

"Said with the wisdom of a matchmaker."

She waited.

"Speaking of that…"

"Of what?"

He tossed a look her way and smiled. Good teeth. Wait. Did she just assess his teeth? That was terrible. But good oral hygiene was a plus in the dating world.

"Speaking of *matchmaking*, I have a problem that I was hoping you could help me with."

"Is that so?"

"My family is driving me crazy."

"Huh."

"My *dat* wants me to learn to farm."

"I thought you were an auctioneer."

"My *bruders* are all up in my business."

"Aggravating."

"But it's my *mamm* that is pushing me over the edge."

Olivia Mae knew that his mother was a sweet,

if concerned, woman. After all, they'd had a good long talk on Monday, when Olivia Mae had taken over a blanket for Sarah's child. The baby wasn't due for another four months, so it had been perhaps obvious that she was making up a reason to visit, but Sarah had been thrilled with the knitted receiving blanket—yellow and green, made from Olivia Mae's own wool, and with a small sheep motif running across the edge.

Of course, she'd picked a morning when she was sure Noah would be at the auction house, and was it her fault that his mother, Erika, had brought up finding a match for Noah? Olivia Mae thought it was a completely natural concern. She might have suggested that Erika make a deal with Noah.

"You're awfully quiet over there," Noah said.

"Am I?"

"Where do sheep take a bath?"

"Let me guess…"

"In a ba-a-athtub," they said together.

She really did need to get him to focus or they'd be here all day. And while his jokes were cute, she had to see to *Daddi* and *Mammi* soon. "You were telling me about your *mamm*."

"She offered me a deal."

"Did she, now?"

"Her deal, or suggestion, is that I give you three chances."

"Excuse me?"

"Three chances to...you know." He twirled his finger in a circle. "Do what you do."

When she only raised her eyebrows, he laughed. "It's like you need to hear me say it."

"I do need to hear you say it. I can't read your mind."

"*Mamm* suggested that if I give you three chances to find me a suitable girl, which I guess you'd be happy to do—"

"Of course I would."

"And if by some chance those three girls don't work out—"

"No reason why one of them wouldn't."

"Then she and *Dat* will leave me alone."

"Leave you alone to—"

"Live my life in peace." This last sentence he practically growled.

Olivia Mae scratched the ewe closest to her between the ears, made her way out of the gate, being careful to latch it securely behind her, and finally turned her attention to Noah.

"I'm not sure that will work."

"What?"

"It sounds as if you're being coerced."

"*Coerced?* Who uses words like that? Did you read them in a book?"

"What book?"

"I don't know what book. I suppose you read *Englisch* romances. That's why you're so keen on this whole true-love business."

"I will admit to having a few sheep magazines as well as some books of knitting patterns. I don't have a lot of time for reading, though I do enjoy it when I have the rare hour to myself. I might have read a novel or two last winter when the weather was too bad to accomplish any work outside."

"Look, I'm not being coerced. I'm being worn down."

"Is there a difference?"

"I don't know."

The look on his face was so miserable that Olivia Mae couldn't help but feel a little pity for him.

"Nice sorrel," she said, walking up to the reddish-brown mare and allowing it to smell her. She then reached into her pocket for a carrot. "What's her name?"

"Snickers—like the candy bar."

She scratched the mare between her ears, causing it to nicker softly.

"Do you do that a lot?"

"What?"

"Take care of things—sheep, horses, people."

He'd stepped closer and she could smell the

soap he'd used, and other things probably from the auction house—old wood and leather and some kind of oil. What was that like? To spend your day selling off people's memories? Maybe she was thinking of it wrongly. Maybe what he did was the ultimate recycling—making old things new again. She looked up at him and smiled, then took a step back.

"What did you mean when you said you're not sure it will work? Would I be such a challenge for you to match up?"

"Most people come to me wanting to find a suitable husband or wife."

"Ya."

"You're practically saying you hope it won't work."

The smile on his face grew. She hadn't known Noah Graber long, but already she knew him well enough to worry when he smiled that way. A girl could fall for that kind of charm, and she made it a point not to harbor romantic feelings about someone she was trying to match.

"You don't think you can do it."

"What?" Her voice came out like a screech owl. She smoothed down her apron and lowered her voice. "Why would you say that?"

"I'm too big a challenge for you."

"Oh, please. I've matched worse—" She almost said *misfits*. "I've matched more stubborn bachelors than you."

"Is that so?"

"It is."

"But younger, I'll bet."

"Matched a thirty-two-year-old last fall."

"Widower?"

"I don't see what difference that makes." She did. Of course she did. The widower had wanted a wife. He was desperately lonely, struggling to raise five children on his own and willing to do whatever she suggested. No need to share all of those details with Noah Graber, though.

"Clearly this is what your *mamm* wants—"

"And my *dat*, my *bruders*, my sisters-in-law—even the bishop."

"Lucas has spoken to you?"

Instead of answering that, he said, "Dating may not be my primary concern, but I'll play along."

"How do I know that you won't sabotage my efforts?"

"Because I'm giving you my word that I won't."

The growl was back. Noah Graber was the full package—tall, handsome, hardworking and with just enough humility to care that he not be called a liar.

She wiped her hands on her apron and then stuck them in her pockets.

"Fine."

"You'll do it?"

"I will."

She began walking toward the house. Noah tagged along beside her, as she'd known he would. Just like teasing a fish with bait, she thought. Good thing *Daddi* had taught her how to fish.

"What happens next?"

She stopped suddenly. "I'll call you."

"You'll call me?"

"Phone shack to phone shack, of course."

"I thought you'd just…give me a name or something."

"I need to think on it, prayerfully consider the situation. You wouldn't want me to rush."

"Kind of, I do." He rolled his eyes when she stared up at him. "As soon as this is over—"

"You'll be able to live your life in peace. I heard you the first time."

"I give you my word that I'm not going to sabotage anything, but you'll see." The grin was back. "I'm not the marrying type."

"You're not?"

"And as soon as this is over, I can get on with my life, establish my reputation as an auctioneer and hopefully make enough to buy a bachelor place."

She could have argued any one of those points. Instead she smiled again—what she hoped was a sincere smile and not one that conveyed how much she'd like to pick up the bucket of water sitting on the front porch and dump it over his head. Anything to erase that condescending grin on his face.

"Great. I'll call when I have some ideas."

And without a backward glance, she hurried up the porch steps and into the house.

Chapter Four

"She still hasn't called?"

Noah and Justin were eating lunch at the Subway sandwich shop in Shipshewana. He had two hours before the next auction, so when his brother had shown up, it had seemed like a good idea. Now he wasn't so sure.

"I already told you that."

"You told me that yesterday."

"And the day before."

"Did you check the recorder at the phone shack today, on your way into work?"

"I did."

"And still nothing?"

"Only a message for Widow King. Something about a crate of baby chicks she'd ordered."

Justin bit into his meatball sub and stared up at the ceiling as he chewed, as if he'd find the answer to their current puzzle written there.

Finally he dropped the sandwich onto the wrapper and admitted, "It only took two days for Olivia Mae to match me with Sarah."

"Two days?"

"Longer for us to court and all, but it only took two days from the time I first visited Olivia Mae. Does she still have that scrawny herd of sheep?"

"If you can call six a herd."

"I wonder what's up with that."

The bell over the door rang and a trio of Amish girls walked in.

"Maybe she needs to cast her net wider." His brother nodded toward the girls. "Plenty of fish here in Shipshe."

"Those aren't fish. They're girls."

"Women."

"And I don't think I specified a geographic location."

"Maybe you should, though. Maybe let her know it doesn't have to be a Goshen girl. Could be we have a shortage or something."

Noah didn't want to talk about his dating life—or his lack of one. He focused on finishing his sandwich, and thought they had moved on from the subject when his brother crossed his arms, sat back and cleared his throat.

"What happened to you?"

"What do you mean?"

"While you were gone. When you were on your extended *rumspringa*..." He waved toward the window. "Wandering all those years."

Noah shrugged. "I don't know what you're asking exactly."

"'Course you do. You just don't want to talk about it."

"If you're so astute, why bother me at all?"

"Because I think you need to talk about it. I think whatever happened out there, it's going to follow you here unless you work through it."

"You sound like Bishop Lucas."

Instead of responding to that, to the fact that their bishop had already asked the same question, Justin plowed on.

"It was hard on *Mamm* and *Dat*, you know—your being gone, them not knowing when or if you were moving back."

"I don't need a lecture from you, little *bruder*."

"And I don't intend to deliver one. Just making sure you're aware."

"Oh, I'm aware."

"*Mamm* probably thinks if you met a girl and married that you'd settle down, that you wouldn't leave again. That's her biggest fear at this point."

"I am settled down—married or single. I'm here to stay, Justin. I'm home, and I don't plan on leaving."

Justin searched his eyes for a minute and apparently found the assurance he needed. "*Gut.* I'd like my son or daughter to know their *onkel* Noah."

With that image planted firmly in his mind, all of Noah's defensiveness melted away. He wanted to be there when Justin's child was born. He wanted to watch all of his nieces and nephews grow up. In truth, he had missed his family more than he'd realized. How many nights had he gone to sleep in a strange town, knowing no one and depending on the kindness of strangers? How many times had he lain there envisioning his father's farm and wishing he was back in Goshen?

His pride had kept him away. He could see that now.

In the end, he'd returned home because he didn't know where else to go, but he was staying because he realized this was where he wanted to be.

They finished their meal, threw their trash onto the tray, dumped it into the nearby trash can and refilled their drinks. Stepping outside, he relaxed. He loved working in Shipshewana, loved how busy it had become and yet it still managed to remain Plain in so many ways.

Sure there were *Englisch* vehicles, but there were also buggies in every direction he looked.

There were *Englisch* tourists—many probably there for the auction—but there were still plenty of Amish folk, as well.

Englisch restaurants abounded, but Jojo's Pretzels and Amish Frozen Custard were as busy as ever.

In short, northern Indiana was what he'd been looking for all along. It was a place where Plain could live beside *Englisch*. They didn't have to worry about ordinances that would require them to diaper their horses. They didn't have to be concerned about becoming less Amish, if there was such a thing.

He could be happy here. He could be content. If only his parents could understand that marriage wasn't for everyone.

If only they'd let him be.

As the brothers were walking back down the road to the auction house, Noah decided maybe Justin would be a good person to vent to. Maybe his brother would realize he was right and tell his mother to cancel the deal they'd made. Already he was regretting it. There had been something about the glint in Olivia Mae's eyes that made him uncomfortable.

It wasn't that he thought she would find the perfect match, but there was a marked look of determination in her eyes. He didn't want to be her pet project.

If he'd been pressed, he would have admitted that he didn't believe there was someone out there for him. Hadn't his past proven that? But between his mother and Olivia Mae, he was in for several weeks, maybe even months, of misery before they understood the futility of what they were attempting to do.

He needed someone on his side—someone who understood his position. Noah glanced back at the sandwich shop and then nudged Justin. "Those girls back there were very young—too young."

"For what?"

"For marrying."

"They looked old enough to me. One was carrying a *boppli*."

"Could have been a niece or nephew."

"They didn't seem too young to me."

"Seventeen, maybe eighteen." Noah jerked the hat off his head and ran his fingers through his hair. "I'm twenty-nine. That's part of the problem."

"Why is that a problem?"

"Because I've never been married before." He rammed the hat back on his head. "I'm like…"

"A freak?"

"An anomaly."

"Whatever."

"Think of me like a horse."

"A horse?"

Noah was warming up to this analogy. His brother had worked around horses all his life. This was something he would be able to relate to and understand.

"Say you found out a horse was for sale, a buggy horse. Only when you went to see it, the horse had never been hitched to a buggy."

"How old is this horse?"

"I don't know. Say it's six years old."

"So a third of its life."

"More or less."

"I get it. You're nearly thirty, which is probably a third of your life."

"Exactly."

"And you've never been hitched to a buggy before."

"Now you understand."

"Is that it?"

"What do you mean?"

"Is that all you've got?"

"I'm just saying there's a reason Olivia Mae hasn't called. There's a reason this whole stupid plan isn't going to work. Old bachelors like myself... Well, young girls aren't interested in us. And everyone else is married."

"What about widows?"

"What about them?"

"Well, every community has a few."

"So you want me to have an instant family?"

"Nothing wrong with it. And the woman would be older, like you and that hypothetical horse."

"Widows are old."

"Not always."

"Even a young widow doesn't want a thirty-year-old who's never—"

"Been hitched to a buggy?"

They'd reached the auction house, and Noah wasn't sure he'd made one bit of progress. His mood plummeted as he realized the uselessness of trying to explain his way of life to his brother. Justin, however, looked thoroughly entertained.

"That was a good story."

"It wasn't a story so much as it was a comparison."

"*Ya.* I get it. I'm just not buying it."

"Meaning…"

"Meaning I know you, and you're hoping that Olivia Mae won't find anyone, but you're also afraid that she will."

With a slap on his back, Justin turned and walked off to where he'd parked his buggy. As Noah headed back into the auction barn, he slowed down to look at the advertisements.

Midwest's Largest Flea Market!
Shipshewana * Trading Place * est. 1922

We love Shipshewana, Indiana, USA
The Heart of Amish Country

He loved everything about the auction house.
It, too, was full of Amish and *Englisch*. He knew
the serious bidders by name, even after less than
three weeks. From the group of *Englischers* he
was able to distinguish between those there to
bid and the ones who were stopping to watch.

Checking in at the office, he made sure of
where he was supposed to be. They had him
scheduled for half a dozen auctions that afternoon—proof that the boss was pleased with his
work. They'd scheduled him in the livestock
barn, which normally he would have enjoyed.
Instead, with every group of animals, he kept
thinking of Olivia Mae's pitiful herd of sheep.

Should he buy her the smaller Dorper sheep?
Their black faces and white wool would make
her smile. Did she even want more sheep? Was
she getting into or out of the business? Why was
he even thinking about her?

The next auction was goats, followed by donkeys. Hadn't she said she'd lost two sheep to
predators? A donkey could help protect her
herd, keep it from dwindling more. Somehow
he continued calling out the bids, joking with
the crowd, moving the animals through the pen,
but his thoughts weren't focused completely on

his work. Instead they pinged around like popcorn in a hot skillet.

Twice he closed a bid while people still had their hands raised. He needed to pay attention, but that wasn't so easy because his mind kept straying back to the woman who was searching for the love of his life. Why had he agreed to his mother's ridiculous deal? Why put himself through the humiliation?

Why hadn't Olivia Mae called?

Before the afternoon was half-done, he'd made up his mind that he'd stop by the phone shack again on the way home. If she hadn't called yet, he'd stop thinking about it. If he was fortunate, maybe she would have decided to call the whole thing off. Whatever Olivia Mae's decision, he was ready to get this over with. Honestly, it was worse than waiting for a dentist appointment.

Olivia Mae waited until Friday to contact Jane, and then she insisted they meet in person. They managed to get together that afternoon. Sitting on the front porch of Jane's home, or rather her parents' home, Olivia Mae couldn't help wondering what eligible man wouldn't want to be a part of her friend's life.

The fields were well tended, the barn in good shape, crops were coming in well and Jane's parents were genuinely nice people. The only problem was they'd had four other daughters, all of whom had married easily and at a young age. They didn't understand what was wrong with their Jane.

That's what her mother had said to Olivia Mae when she'd arrived at the house. "Are you here to set her up? Because we don't understand what's wrong with our Jane." The woman's demeanor suggested nothing but parental love. The family didn't fight, no one had a drug or alcohol problem, and none of the girls had gone through much of a *rumspringa*. Olivia Mae knew this firsthand because she'd gone to school with all of the older girls. Jane, being six years younger, had been in second grade the year that Olivia Mae had finished eighth.

She pushed away that uncomfortable thought.

After assuring Jane's mother that there was nothing wrong with Jane, she'd waited on the front porch. Best to do this away from curious ears, even if those ears were well-meaning.

Twenty minutes later, Jane had joined her and listened to her suggestions, but she still wasn't convinced.

"I thought he wasn't interested," Jane repeated.

They'd been through this once, but apparently Olivia Mae's assurances hadn't calmed her fears.

"It's his *mamm*'s idea for him to allow me to try to make a match, but Noah agreed to it. If he agreed to it, then I think somewhere in his heart he wants it."

Jane nodded, but she didn't answer right away. Jane was a talker, so Olivia Mae wasn't sure how to interpret her silence. She repeatedly smoothed the apron covering her dress, and finally turned and looked at Olivia Mae directly.

"Is this it?"

"What do you mean?"

"Is it my last chance?"

"Of course not."

"Because I'm twenty-one."

"I'm twenty-seven." Olivia Mae tried not to take offense. It was true that most in their community considered someone past the age of twenty-five to be a late bloomer. And thirty? Well, by thirty most people simply accepted that the loved one wouldn't ever marry. Noah was dangerously close to that age, but Olivia Mae wasn't going to let that stop her.

"It's only that my *schweschdern*, they all married young, and my *mamm*, she worries. I even heard her talking to my *dat* the other night, asking how I would run the farm when they're gone, as if they're going to stride through the pearly gates any day now. They're not even sick. They're only in their fifties, and many people live to be older than that. Widow King turned ninety-one this year, and I think she's related to us in some convoluted way. Once my *mamm* told me…"

This was the Jane that Olivia Mae knew—a chatterbox with a propensity to worry. It was something they were working on. Olivia Mae sat forward and claimed Jane's hands in her own.

"Take a deep breath."

"Okay." She inhaled.

"Blow it out."

She rolled her eyes, but did as requested and exhaled.

"Relax your shoulders."

As she did, she sat up straighter and set the rocker slowly in motion.

"Feel better?"

"Ya."

"Jane, I know what it is like to be Amish. I am Amish. I understand the pressure you feel, but I want you to understand your worth as a person—as a single woman. *Gotte* has a plan and a purpose for your life, whether it includes a husband and children or not."

"I know." Her voice was small, tentative. She bowed her head and pulled in a deep breath, and then sat up even straighter. "I know that. I believe that, it's only…it's only that I want a husband and I want children."

"*Wunderbaar.* If that is the desire of your heart, then I believe that *Gotte* will provide a way." As an afterthought, she added, "But let's not spring all of that on Noah at once."

Jane nodded, and then she began to laugh, and then Olivia Mae started laughing. It took five minutes to pull the conversation back on course.

"I'll call Noah day after tomorrow."

"Sunday?"

"*Ya.*"

"Not tonight?"

"*Nein.* I think it would be better if we wait. I'd rather your first date not be on a Friday or Saturday."

"Okay." Jane didn't ask why.

Olivia Mae understood that in matters of the *when* and *where* and *how* of dating, the girls she worked with trusted her to make good decisions.

"I think Tuesday would be good."

"Next Tuesday?"

"Less than a week away."

"That's true. What should I wear?"

"Your favorite thing, the thing that makes you smile when you pull it off the hanger."

"I only have four dresses and five aprons, but I do have that sweater you knitted me..."

"From the variegated blue yarn. It's light-weight and it matches your eyes nicely."

"I hardly ever wear it. I don't want people to think I'm putting on airs, but if we go out Tuesday night, well, there is a chill in the air on May evenings."

"Indeed there is."

Olivia Mae stood and started down the steps. When she looked back at Jane, she realized suddenly how much she liked her, how in some ways Jane and all the women she helped seemed like the younger sisters she'd never had. So instead of leaving, she walked back up the steps and squatted in front of Jane.

"We don't know—we can't know—if Noah is the man that *Gotte* intends for you."

Surprisingly Jane didn't interrupt.

"But we do know He has a plan, and we can trust Him. So Tuesday night, remember this isn't on you. It's not about what you do right or wrong. It's about finding out if Noah Graber is the man that *Gotte* intends for you to marry, and maybe you won't even know that right away. But I want you to just enjoy yourself, okay?"

For her answer, Jane leaned forward and enfolded Olivia Mae in a hug, reminding her again of the sister she'd never had.

Chapter Five

Olivia Mae loved that they only had church every other Sunday. On the off Sundays, she missed the hymns and the prayers and even the singing. But she loved the extra time that they had to rest and simply be with one another. Plus the gatherings on their off Sundays were usually small.

She didn't have to call Noah to tell him about his upcoming date because they ended up at the same family gathering on Sunday—this time at Bishop Lucas's house. Since *Mammi* and *Daddi* had no other relatives in the area, they often spent the Sundays when they didn't have church at the bishop's. It had started with Atlee and continued with Lucas. Olivia Mae was a tad surprised to see Noah and his family there, but she shouldn't have been. It was just that he had such a large family, so she figured they'd always meet at his parents' house.

"My *bruders* are spread out," he explained. "Samuel, Justin and George live here, but it was their week to visit their in-laws. My other two *bruders* live in Middlebury—close enough to visit a few times a month, but not usually on a Sunday."

"Which means your parents were home alone."

"Not completely. I was there." He grinned at her sheepishly. "But I'm not the best company."

"And why is that?"

"I don't want to hear the stories they've told a hundred times. I'd rather be up and moving about than sitting in a rocker. Every conversation seems to lead to a lecture. Take your pick of reasons."

They were walking through the bishop's back pasture. Olivia Mae was picking a bouquet of wildflowers—tiny clumps of blue-eyed Mary, the occasional pasture rose with its yellow center and something her mother had called bird's-foot violet. The memory made her smile. How she missed her parents, but it seemed that reminders of them were everywhere.

She gathered the flowers for *Mammi*, who claimed to enjoy the sight and smell of them. The small bouquets certainly brightened up the house considerably, and they cost nothing. Their house could use some brightening. Three new holes in the roof had shown up with the last rainstorm. Olivia Mae needed to think of a way to fix that, or she could hope they wouldn't have any more pouring rains. The lighter showers didn't seem to work their way through the roof.

"Where did you go?" Noah asked.

"Go?"

"I lost you there for a minute. I was complaining about my parents in a very entertaining way and you just…" He interlocked his thumbs and mimed a bird flying away.

Instead of boring him with details of how her grandparents' home was falling apart, she opted to change the subject.

"I was trying to think how best to tell you that I have a date for you."

He stopped in the middle of the field and crossed his arms. She thought that would make a pretty picture, if she had a camera or could even sketch. Most Amish didn't own a camera, though of course some on their *rumspringa* did. Sketching was allowed, but any artists among them usually stuck to landscapes. Still, Olivia Mae couldn't help thinking that Noah Graber looked like something in a picture, in his Sunday best, crossing his arms—a scowl on his face and wildflowers at his feet.

"We've been talking for a while. You could have led with that."

"Her name is Jane. She is a friend of mine."

"One of the girls you were sitting with?"

"Yes."

"Tall or chubby?"

She fisted her hands on her hips and scowled at him. "If that's your attitude…"

"I'm kidding. Relax. You take this thing very seriously, you know."

He walked over to a bunch of buttercups, pulled three out of the ground and handed them to her. "Peace offering?"

"I'm serious, Noah." She accepted the flowers, but kept her gaze on him. "These women are *freinden* of mine, and they deserve your respect."

"Why are women so sensitive?" The expression on his face told her that it was a serious question. "If we were looking at horses, it would be okay for me to ask about the tall one or the chubby one."

"Women are not horses."

"When I'm auctioning items, it's okay for me to describe things in details. It's what I'm supposed to do."

"But you would say *antique*, not *old*. You would say *lovingly worn*, not *falling apart*. You would speak kindly."

He grunted in reply.

They crossed the pasture and stopped at the fence line, where more flowers grew in abundance. It was a fine May day, and Olivia Mae should feel happy and excited that she'd found a possible match for Noah, and for Jane. Instead she felt worried.

"Jane is tall, yes."

"Do you know how many times I've been set up with the tall *schweschder*?"

"I wasn't aware you'd ever been set up before."

"When I was younger. Everyone seemed to think that tall people wanted to be around other tall people—like we were a tribe or something."

Olivia Mae craned her head back to get a good look at his face. "Do you dislike being tall?"

"Of course not. What good would it do? A giraffe doesn't dislike having a long neck."

"A giraffe?" She shook her head at the absurdity of their conversations. "Let's refocus. Jane is self-conscious about her height."

"She didn't look that tall."

"And yet beside other women, she's always the tallest, and some men—I won't mention names—have said disparaging things, perhaps because they were short and felt uncomfortable beside her."

"I won't call her Big Bird."

"Did you watch a lot of *Englisch* television as a child?"

"*Nein*. But I helped to build an addition on to a day-care center once, and just before nap time they'd play shows for the kids. Kind of gets stuck in your head."

"Another *gut* reason not to have a television."

"We can agree on that."

"Jane is available to go out with you on Tuesday."

"I thought you'd say Friday. Don't most dates take place on Friday?"

"Tuesday works better." She didn't explain her reasoning. "I suggest you take her to dinner in town."

"I'm not made of money, you know."

"You're living with your parents, and you're earning money at the auction house."

"True enough, but I'm saving up for my own place. It seems a waste of good money to go out to dinner when I could…"

"What? Let Jane cook for you?"

"I didn't—"

"Or maybe you'd planned on rustling up a meal on your own."

"That would be a terrible idea. I've been known to burn toast."

"Did you want to take her home to your parents and let your *mamm* cook for her?"

"*Nein. Mamm*'s a *gut* cook, but she'd be asking her about *grandkinner* before we made it to dessert." Noah scrubbed a hand across his face. "This is the problem with dating. There are too many details."

He looked truly frustrated—almost miserable if she wasn't mistaken, and that was not the way she wanted this date to begin. So she reached out and touched his arm. He stared down at her hand, then into her eyes.

Olivia Mae jerked her hand away, feeling as if she'd dared to touch a hot stove. "Dating can feel overwhelming at first. Think of it as an investment."

He snorted.

"If you want a relationship you have to be willing to spend the time and a little money."

"Fine."

"And it's a chance to enjoy yourself. You work hard. One dinner out a week isn't such an extravagance."

"We're supposed to do this every week?"

She hoped he was kidding, but one look at his face told her he was quite serious.

Olivia Mae jerked a few more flowers out of the ground, decided her bouquet was large enough and turned back toward the group of old folks enjoying the May afternoon. "Let's just deal with this one week at a time. Take Jane somewhere that you like. It'll help her to learn more about you."

She pulled a piece of paper out of her pocket and handed it to him. "Pick her up at five thirty."

She'd written Jane's name, address and the number to the nearest phone shack. At the bottom she'd penciled in a list of things to remember and added a note that read "Girls love flowers." It was what she did with every new match. Sometimes men needed a little prodding in the right direction. She had a feeling Noah Graber was going to require something much more obvious, like a good solid push.

Noah had thrown away Olivia Mae's list. Who needed instructions on how to go on a date? He wasn't a child. Noah had left home feeling confident that a relationship with Jane wouldn't work, but for mysterious reasons, not because he was going to mess it up. He did not plan to sabotage this. In fact, he thought that he'd done everything right.

Maybe Olivia Mae didn't know what she was doing, because he'd certainly met her expectations. He'd done it all except for the flowers, which, honestly, he had forgotten completely about.

Pick Jane up on Tuesday night—check.
Take Jane to his favorite place—check.

Don't mention Jane's height—check!

So why had the night felt like such a failure? Who was he kidding? It didn't just feel like a failure, it *was* a failure. He could tell as much by the way that Jane had stopped attempting to make conversation and sat quietly in the buggy with her hands clutched in her lap. When he had pulled up to her parents' house, she had murmured "good night" while still staring at her hands and literally fled inside without a backward glance.

He'd stewed over the situation while he was at work on Wednesday.

He'd vowed he wouldn't think about it while he worked around the farm on Thursday.

But on Friday he couldn't stand it any longer. This was Olivia Mae's fault. Why did people think she was a *wunderbaar* matchmaker? She was terrible! She was probably too embarrassed to call him, so it was up to him to call her—or better yet, stop by after work and see her.

It occurred to him as he rode the bus back to Goshen that perhaps he was worrying for nothing. Just maybe Olivia Mae would be ready to admit defeat and call off the entire deal. He changed into his everyday clothes and hitched up the buggy. Maybe she was ready to surrender! That thought cheered him immensely as he drove the buggy toward her house.

Olivia Mae was in the pasture tending to her buggy horse when he arrived. Standing ten feet away, looking dolefully at what she was doing, was a brown jenny mule. Good thing he hadn't bought her one of the donkeys at the auction.

He'd planned to start right in on discussing the date, but instead he asked, "Why the mule?"

Olivia Mae glanced up, then turned her attention back to the horse, brushing through its mane and stroking it with her other hand. "We only have the one horse."

"So?"

"Horses are social animals. This one was showing signs of depression."

"Horses get depressed?"

Instead of answering, she asked, "Are you sure you grew up Amish?"

He waved away her question. "That date you set me up on was a disaster."

"So I heard."

"What's that supposed to mean?"

"Jane came by Wednesday morning."

"And said what? I did everything that you told me to do."

"Oh, really?" She pointed the currycomb at him. "You promised me you wouldn't intentionally mess this up."

"I didn't."

He jerked his straw hat off his head, slapped it against his leg and then put it back on.

"I did not intentionally mess anything up," he said in a calmer voice. "Like every other date I've been on, it seemed to start out okay and then slid rapidly downhill."

"Maybe we should talk about your dating history."

"Maybe we shouldn't." He walked away from her then, because he couldn't stand the look of confusion on her face.

He didn't want to explain about Cora or Samantha or Ida.

Three different women from three different states.

Three different relationships that he thought might have been the one.

Three different kinds of disaster.

He didn't want to relive the humiliation and regret and guilt. He was home now and those experiences were behind him. All he wanted was a fresh start. All he wanted to do was be an auctioneer.

Of course, he had agreed to only three dates.

Maybe he was looking at this all wrong. Maybe he should be relieved the date with Jane was such a disaster. Two more nights of humiliation and his family would leave him alone. He'd be free to pursue his dream of being a successful auctioneer without wasting time and money on something that wasn't ever going to happen. He could start searching for his bachelor pad. In fact, he should purchase a paper on the way home and scan the for-sale ads. The thought cheered him immensely.

He turned back toward the pasture, nearly plowed into Olivia Mae and took a step back. "Didn't realize you were done with the horse."

"Why don't we go to the porch, have some lemonade and talk about this?"

He wasn't sure he liked the idea of having an extended conversation about Tuesday night. Then again, the thought of sitting on the front porch with Olivia Mae sipping fresh lemonade didn't sound terrible.

Glancing at her, he realized that she looked tired and a little defeated. Where was the spunky girl he'd met when he first brought over the letter box? Maybe the situation with her grandparents was difficult emotionally and physically. Maybe she needed to go out on a date—take a teaspoonful of her own medicine. The thought brought a smile to his lips, and then he remembered one of the jokes he'd memorized for her.

"Why was the sheep arrested on the freeway?"

"Oh, Noah…"

"Because she did a ewe-turn."

She didn't laugh out loud, but he thought maybe her shoulders looked less bunched up. That animal-joke book he'd bought in the gift shop next to the auction house was definitely worth what he'd paid for it.

Olivia Mae's grandmother insisted on bringing them two large glasses of lemonade as well as a plate of cookies.

"Danki," he said.

"Gem Gschehne." She smiled broadly at him, the skin around her eyes folding into a patchwork of wrinkles. He could see the similarity then—between Olivia Mae and Rachel. Their eyes were shaped the same and they both had brilliant smiles. "I hope you're enjoying Goshen."

"Oh, *ya*. I like Goshen fine." He almost added, "it's the meddling I hate," but since it was her granddaughter in charge of the meddling, that might sound a bit rude. So instead he raised the glass, sipped the cold drink and smacked his lips together. *"Gut* lemonade."

"Olivia Mae made it. She's a *wunderbaar* cook. You should try her fried chicken."

"Actually I had some at the church luncheon."

"And her pot roast is *gut*, too. Then there's the cakes she bakes—"

"Stop talking about me as if I'm not sitting right here." Olivia Mae nodded toward the living room. "*Danki* for the drinks, *Mammi*. We don't want to keep you from what you were doing."

Instead of being offended, her *mammi* laughed and said, "That's my signal to leave."

When she'd gone inside, he noticed the melancholy expression return to Olivia Mae's face. "Your *mammi* seems very nice."

"She's the best. Both her and *Daddi* are."

Suddenly she wouldn't look at him directly. Something was up, but he couldn't imagine what it was. The older couple seemed healthy enough from what he'd seen of them on Sunday. Was there something she hadn't shared yet? Why was she living here alone with her grandparents? And how hard was that?

Did Olivia Mae have trouble asking for help?

"Where do your parents live?"

"They died—ten years ago in a car accident." She rubbed the heel of her palm against her chest, though she seemed unaware that she was doing it. "You hear how dangerous buggies are, but they were in a van that they'd hired to take them to see relatives in the southern part of the state. An oncoming vehicle crossed the line, pushing them into a concrete barrier. They were killed instantly."

"I'm so sorry." It sounded like a stupid thing to say, and he regretted it immediately.

"Their life was complete."

She smoothed out the apron over her dress. It was a somber gray. He wondered why she always dressed like that. The blue sweater that Jane had worn on their date would have looked beautiful on Olivia Mae. Hadn't Jane told her that Olivia Mae had made it? Yet her own clothing was always so...plain. He pushed the thought from his mind, choosing to focus on the beautiful May afternoon, the sheep in the pasture in front of them and the tart sweetness of the lemonade.

Olivia Mae had other ideas. "Let's go back over what happened."

"I don't see how that will help."

"When did you pick Jane up?"

"Before dinner, like you said. I guess it was..." He stared up at the roof of the porch. "Six, maybe six thirty. Could have been closer to seven."

"We agreed on five thirty."

"What difference does it make?"

"The difference it makes is that Jane was sitting on her front porch waiting for you for nearly an hour and a half. That's a long time for her to wonder if you had perhaps changed your mind."

"I would never do that."

"Punctuality is a sign of respect."

"Look, I would have been on time, but my *dat* insisted that I walk out with him to look at the fields. He's clinging to the long-cherished idea that I'm going to wake up one day and have a sudden desire to take up farming. By the time we got back to the house, and I changed clothes and harnessed the horse, it was already six thirty. Then I lost the sheet with her directions and had to go back inside and ask my *mamm* for directions."

"You could have told your *dat* that you had other plans and that you'd be happy to go with him in the fields another time."

"I guess. In truth, it's easier to tag along when he asks rather than argue with him." He honestly did not see what the big deal was, and he said as much to Olivia Mae, but she started shaking her head before he was even finished.

"What time does your auction begin?"

"What?"

"Your auction. What time does it start?"

"What does that have to do with my dating?"

"Just humor me."

"I had three on Monday and four on Wednesday. Today I had nine." He couldn't help feeling proud that the auction house was giving him more responsibility, and he was relieved that Olivia Mae had moved on to a different subject. Talking about work was easier than discussing his feelings about dating. "On Mondays my lots start at ten, two and four."

"On the nose?"

"What? *Ya.* Of course. It would be unprofessional to start late."

Instead of responding, she stared at him, eyebrows raised, like a schoolteacher who was waiting for him to catch on to a lesson.

He dropped his head into his hands and tried to replay her words in his mind. But instead of hearing what she'd said, he kept seeing her watching him, that small smile playing across her pink lips. Finally he glanced up and admitted, "I have no idea what point you're trying to make."

"Noah, think about it. You would never consider starting an auction late because it would be rude to the people coming to bid on the items."

"Eventually they'd stop coming to my auctions, then I wouldn't sell anything, and soon after that I'd be fired."

"Exactly. In the same way it's rude to show up an hour and a half late for a date."

"But a date isn't an auction." He guzzled the rest of the lemonade and then growled, "Women are so different from men."

"Why do you say that?"

"I wouldn't care if my brother showed up late to go fishing."

"Then perhaps women are different than men."

She took another sip of the lemonade, and he suddenly wondered what it would be like to kiss her.

Whoa.

Where had that come from?

She was the matchmaker, not the match.

"Why aren't you married?"

"What?" Olivia Mae's eyes widened.

"No offense, but if you're so good at this, why aren't you married yourself? Why haven't you found *your* perfect match?"

"We're not talking about me right now. We're talking about you. Now, why did you take her to a gas station for dinner?"

"It wasn't a gas station! Well, I mean they do sell gas, but they also have a *wunderbaar* barbecue place on the side. It's this little trailer, and there are wooden benches set up on the concrete pad—"

She held up a hand to stop him. "Most women don't enjoy eating at an establishment that sells fuel—"

"What does that have to do with the price of oats?"

"They want a nice dinner out or a romantic picnic."

"A romantic picnic?" He snorted. "How is

eating in a park on a blanket romantic? At least we had an actual table to sit at."

"Let's move on."

"*Ya.* Let's."

"Apparently you talked to her about your auctioneering. You talked about that a lot, but you never asked her a single question about what she does during the day."

"Did she write you a report and hand it to you?"

"Don't get defensive."

"Of course I'm defensive. I didn't ask Jane any questions because I didn't want to seem nosy."

"When you ask questions about someone, you're showing an interest in them, not being nosy."

Noah slammed his cup of lemonade down on the table, grateful that neither was made of glass, and jumped up out of the rocker. He walked over to the porch railing, attempted a few shoulder rolls to loosen the knots in his muscles and tried to figure out how to call off this entire fiasco.

Why had he ever made such a stupid agreement with his mother? And how was he going to endure two more nights of humiliation? But it was only two nights.

Only two more women who would most certainly reject him.

So instead of explaining how unreasonable she was being, he turned to Olivia Mae with a smile pasted on his face. Leaning against the railing, he jerked off his hat, crossed his arms and said, "Okay. Be on time. No gas station. Ask questions. Got it. When do I take her out again?"

"It's not that simple."

"What do you mean?"

"Jane...doesn't think that you're compatible."

"How can she know that after one date?" He felt his cheeks burning and knew that he was blushing. He rammed the hat back on his head, hoping that Olivia Mae wouldn't notice. "How am I supposed to get better at this if she won't give me another chance?"

"We try with someone else."

"The chubby...er, wait. Don't give me that lecture again. The other girl that you were sitting with at our church meeting?"

"Her name is Francine, and yes—that is who I had in mind."

Noah ran his hand over his face. Two more dates, and he would have fulfilled his half of the bargain. "Okay. I'm in."

"Tomorrow night."

"That soon?"

"Sure. I don't want you to have time to forget what you learned."

He wouldn't forget, but he also knew it wouldn't matter.

She pulled another sheet of paper from her pocket. It looked just like the first one she'd given him. Same precise handwriting. Same list. Same smiley face at the bottom. What grown-up put a smiley face on the bottom of a note? It didn't matter. He didn't even need her instructions, but he stared at the paper, folded it up neatly and stuck it in his pocket all the same.

If Olivia Mae understood what she was up against, how many times he'd crashed and burned in the dating arena, she would surrender now. But she was as stubborn as he was, and he could tell by the look on her face that she would see this through to the bitter end.

He forced his voice to be pleasant. No use letting her see how crazy she was making him. "Fine."

"Really?"

"Sure. You're the matchmaker."

He walked back to his buggy whistling. Something would go wrong tomorrow night. He didn't know how he knew, but he did. Then Olivia Mae would search around for one more poor girl to throw his way, and he'd mess that up, too. This entire foolish plan to find him a wife would be over by the following week.

As he drove away, he glanced back and saw Olivia Mae standing on the porch, watching his buggy…or maybe watching him. He didn't know why he didn't tell her the truth—that Jane seemed like a nice young girl, but a girl. Why didn't anyone seem to realize he was nearly thirty years old? He didn't want to date someone who was barely out of their *rumspringa*.

He wanted to date someone who had a little experience in life, who understood that there was more to a person than the condition of their buggy or whether they arrived on time or not. He wanted to date someone who wasn't out looking for love but was involved in their own life—caring for others, pursuing their dreams, content whether they found a spouse or not.

What he wanted was to date someone like Olivia Mae.

Ha. Not likely. She could give sage advice, but didn't seem to be interested in following it.

Nein. Dating Olivia Mae wasn't going to happen.

She hadn't shown the least bit of interest in him—other than as a puzzle she needed to solve.

Still, he warmed up to the idea as he drove home. Someone like Olivia Mae was what would suit him best. He knew it—felt it in his heart. Didn't he feel more comfortable with her? And they had things to talk about. He didn't have to have a list of topics penned on his palm like he'd done the other night.

Olivia Mae was more his style.

Perhaps he should ask if she had a twin sister hiding somewhere.

Chapter Six

Olivia Mae knew that Jane had already spoken with Francine about Noah. She could have left her a message at the phone shack telling her about the date she'd set up for her with Noah. Somehow a phone message seemed too impersonal, though, plus there was the fact that it was happening in a few hours. They'd talked about the possibility, but Olivia Mae had promised to get back to her with the exact details. She wanted a chance to meet with Francine and answer any questions. It wouldn't hurt to calm her nerves a bit. So she'd left a message saying she'd like to see her the next morning, and they'd decided on a girls' trip to town.

They were at the thrift store in Goshen as soon as it opened Saturday morning. This particular store supported Habitat for Humanity, which Olivia Mae had heard a lot of good things about. The person who had told her about their work building houses for those in need was an older man who worked for Mennonite Disaster Services. Olivia Mae had once thought about going on MDS missions herself, but now with her grandparents' health worsening every day that wasn't going to happen.

Mammi had warned her earlier that morning about traveling alone to Goshen even though they lived in Goshen. She'd acted as if their farm was miles and miles away from anyone else. She'd acted as if they lived in the old days, when the Plain community was small and folks lived farther apart.

And as Olivia Mae had walked out the front door, Rachel had reminded her to stop at the apothecary for her herbs. Apothecary? Had they ever had one of those? Was her *mammi* losing it completely? Or was she simply confused? Maybe she'd even been misheard. Regardless, Olivia Mae didn't think that she'd be going on an MDS mission any time soon.

She caught up with Francine, who was looking for anything that she could cut up for quilt squares. She loved making salvage or, the more popular term, *scrappy* quilts. She would purchase curtains, sheets, even old clothes to cut into squares and triangles. Francine was an excellent quilter. Olivia Mae preferred to knit. She liked visiting thrift stores because she could sometimes find sweaters for a quarter, frog the yarn, wash it and make something brand-new.

"Frog?" Francine asked. "What does that even mean?"

"It's the sound you make when you—you know. Rip the yarn out."

Francine began to giggle, and Olivia Mae was reminded of Noah's silly sheep jokes. In one way, those terrible jokes proved that he had a caring personality—at least he seemed to care about making her laugh. She thought he was probably a very kind person, only nervous when it came to women. She remembered his red ears the night before and how he'd tried to cover them with his hat. Nervous and easily embarrassed—both qualities that she thought were endearing in a man.

The question was whether Francine would feel the same way.

They finished pawing through the bins, paid for their purchases and walked out into a perfect May afternoon.

"Let's sit for a minute—if you have time."

"Sure." Francine plopped onto the wooden bench, dropped her bags near her feet and turned toward Olivia Mae. "I guess you want to give me some tips, so my evening with Noah doesn't end in disaster like Jane's did."

"She told you about that?"

"Described every agonizing moment."

Olivia Mae fought to hold in a sigh and failed. "Perhaps it's best if you just forget all of that and give Noah a chance."

"Oh, I plan to. I don't care if we eat at a gas station."

"You won't be."

"Or even if he's late. What's the big deal?"

Maybe Francine was a better match, or maybe she was simply trying very hard to appear to be.

"It's okay to expect someone to be on time, you know."

"*Ya*, I know." She fiddled with the strings of her prayer *kapp* and stared out at the passing traffic—cars, horses pulling buggies and folks riding bicycles.

Goshen had certainly grown, even in the few years since Olivia Mae had moved there. *Mammi*'s earlier comments about the apothecary pushed into her mind, twisting her heart, but she shook her head and focused on Francine.

"I don't even mind listening to details about the auction. Anything different from the same old thoughts circling through my mind would be *gut*."

Francine lived with her *bruder* and his family. It was a crowded home with nine children. She'd confessed to Olivia Mae that often she retreated into her own thoughts, completely un-aware of what was going on around her. It was a form of self-preservation, according to Fran-cine. Otherwise the sheer number of children in the house would overwhelm her.

She also struggled with diabetes, which she'd been diagnosed with as a young teenager. It was hard to avoid carbohydrates in an Amish home, especially one full of children. Francine was very serious about her health, especially since she had an overactive sweet tooth. The two chal-lenges—a love for sweets and diabetes—were a constant battle for her. Living in a houseful of children only made that worse.

Olivia Mae knew there were plenty of fami-lies with more than ten children, but she sus-pected that it was easier if you added one at a time. Francine had moved from another state to be with her *bruder*. Her family had hoped it would increase her dating prospects. So far, it hadn't done much more than cause Francine to question whether she ever wanted to have chil-dren. She'd once confessed she didn't want to take care of another thing—person, pet or plant.

"Jane is thinking of writing to Elijah," Fran-cine said.

"What?"

"Ya."

"She told you that?"

"She did." Francine glanced at Olivia Mae and then back at the street. "She said that the date with Noah opened her eyes. She doesn't need a perfect man, but she does need someone who is interested in her. That was her exact word—*interested*."

"Whatever does that mean? Of course Noah was interested. He's just out of practice as far as relating to women."

Francine was tapping her fingertips against her lips, as if she wasn't sure she should say what she wanted to say. Finally she shrugged and looked directly at Olivia Mae. "Jane said he wasn't interested and that she could tell. He was, you know…only going through the motions."

"She said that?"

"I know what she means." Francine sighed and rubbed at her elbow. She'd admitted the previous week that the hand-quilting tended to cause the joints in her right arm to ache. "My *bruder* set me up with one of his buddies once—this was before I knew you. It didn't go well, and it left me feeling like a shelter dog that no one wanted. He never looked directly at me, and it seemed he couldn't get me home quickly enough."

Just when Olivia Mae thought she knew all that these young girls had been through, she unpeeled another layer. "I'm sorry that happened to you, but Noah isn't like that. He's just shy, and he doesn't think there's anyone out there for him. It's not that he's uninterested, he's simply not a believer in romantic love."

When Francine didn't respond, she said, "Do you think Jane will do it? Write Elijah?"

"She might. She told me that she realizes it doesn't matter what he does for a living—that details like that will work themselves out. What matters is how they feel about one another, and she's beginning to realize how much she did care for him." She pulled more tightly on her *kapp* strings. "And before you say that she's confusing loneliness for affection, I think she might be right."

Olivia Mae sighed and stood up, gathering up the two paper bags full of sweaters she'd purchased. It would be enough yarn to last her at least a month.

"What do you think?" Francine asked.

"I think our Jane is growing up, and I think you need to head home so you'll be ready for your date with Noah."

Olivia Mae expected to go home and spend the afternoon worrying over Noah's date, but she never had the chance. She pulled into the yard and saw *Mammi* pacing on the front porch.

"What's wrong?"

"It's your *daddi*."

"Is he all right?"

"I don't know. I don't know where he is."

"Tell me what happened." She clasped her *mammi*'s hand in hers. They were cold, and it was obvious she'd been crying. "Why don't you sit down, here in the rocker. Take a deep breath. It's going to be all right."

When *Mammi* didn't answer, she reached out and tucked her hand under the dear woman's chin, forcing her to look up. "Do you believe me?"

"I suppose." The answer was a whisper, a prayer.

"*Gut*. Now tell me what happened."

"He was napping, in his chair. I thought I had enough time before he woke, so I went outside to work in the garden. When I came back inside, he was gone."

"And you've looked in the barn?"

"*Ya*."

"And the pasture?"

"*Ya*, of course. I thought of running to the phone shack, but then… Well, what if he came back and no one was here and he got scared?"

"It's okay, *Mammi*. You did the right thing to wait here."

"I did?"

"*Ya*."

Mammi closed her eyes, clasped her hands

and began to silently pray. Olivia Mae knew that was what she was doing because her breathing evened out and she slowly began to put the rocking chair into motion, plus she'd seen her do that very thing a hundred times before—maybe a thousand times. And wasn't prayer what they needed at a time like this? Surely *Gotte* would help them to find *Daddi*. She added her own prayers to her grandmother's, and then she turned toward the still-harnessed horse. That wouldn't work, though, because *Daddi* probably would not stick to the road. He'd wandered off before and it was always across a pasture, as he would forget where their land ended and another farm began.

Olivia Mae reached out and covered *Mammi*'s hands with her own. "I'm going to the barn."

Mammi's eyes popped open. "But the horse and buggy are right here."

"I need to take my bike. Can you unhitch Zeus?"

"Of course."

"Just leave the buggy here. I'll put it up later, and if you open the pasture gate, Zeus will follow you in."

"I know how to pasture the horse."

And there was a small miracle, because she could see in her grandmother's face that she did remember how and would be able to do it.

The confusion of the morning and the panic of a few moments ago had both passed.

Olivia Mae broke into a run. The last thing she wanted to do was explain to *Mammi* that she didn't think *Daddi* would stay on the road. She'd be better off with the bicycle. She'd start at his favorite fishing spot—though he hadn't fished in over a year—then work her way around to the neighbors. If she didn't find him by dark, she'd call Lucas.

She prayed that wouldn't happen.

She prayed that *Daddi* was all right, that he'd simply sat down somewhere and was resting.

She prayed that she wasn't too late.

Noah thought that he'd done better.

He'd picked up a couple of cans of soda, some fried chicken, a bag of chips and a package of cookies while he was in town running errands for his *mamm*. Olivia Mae might be right about some things, but he thought she was wrong about choosing restaurants. Who wanted to eat in a noisy restaurant on a Saturday? The weather was beautiful, and Olivia Mae had mentioned romantic picnics in an offhand way. No doubt she thought that was beyond him, but the bag of groceries behind his seat proved she was wrong.

He arrived twenty minutes early, which for some reason seemed to fluster Francine.

Then he drove her to the park, which was where the trouble began.

"This is where we're eating?"

"*Ya.* I thought it would be nice to enjoy the beautiful weather."

The park was full of children of all ages, plus quite a few dogs. It looked to him like everyone was having a good time, and he silently congratulated himself on having such a good idea. Hopefully the natural setting would help them relax around one another.

"Where are we going to sit?"

He'd thought there would be picnic tables, but there weren't. He glanced into the back seat of the buggy and spied his old horse blanket. It would do.

He handed her the bag of groceries, then fastened the mare to the buggy post and went to the back seat to pull out the blanket. They walked down to the pond and he shook the dirt from the blanket, then laid it on the ground.

Francine had eyed the blanket suspiciously, but she sat down without comment. When he began pulling out their food, her eyes grew rounder.

"This is what we're eating?"

"*Ya.* Fried chicken is *gut*, and who doesn't like chips and cookies?"

"Oh." She seemed to think about that for a minute. Finally she shrugged and asked, "Do you have plates or silverware?"

"Don't need it, not really." He popped the top on a can of soda and handed it to her. She stared at the drink as if it was a snake, then set it down in the grass and said, "I'm not very hungry, but *danki*."

He had asked her about her day, and paid attention when she described her quilting. He learned what a scrappy quilt was, and how salvage quilting was a type of recycling, and even that nine squares in a certain order made it a nine-patch. He felt Francine was a virtual encyclopedia of quilting terms, and he was a student trying to catch up.

But the problems cropped up pretty quickly. They seemed to be opposites. He sensed it almost immediately, and he thought she did, too.

Francine couldn't wait to put Goshen behind her. Noah was glad to be home.

Francine was pretty sure she didn't want any children, or at least not very many. Noah had always imagined himself with a houseful of kids—when he imagined himself as anything other than an old crotchety bachelor.

Francine jumped if any of the dogs came near

them. Noah thought he wouldn't mind having one when he bought his own place.

Worse yet—she didn't like his jokes. She had stared at him when he'd shared one about pigs.

What do you call a pig with no legs?

A ground-hog.

Hilarious!

But Francine only chewed on her thumbnail and glanced away.

He was going to say, "Even Olivia Mae would have laughed at that one," but at the last second decided to keep that comment to himself.

Then the mosquitos attacked. He slapped one that was feasting on her arm and left a trail of blood. "Guess that one already got you."

"*Ya.* I guess it did." She looked around for a napkin to wipe off her arm, but he didn't have any. She'd settled for a corner of the horse blanket, which left a red rash on her arm.

But the biggest blunder of the evening had come when he took her home. He parked at the corner of the house, where the light from the living room couldn't reach them. It wasn't quite dark, but the sun was setting. Now, this was what Olivia Mae would call a romantic moment, or so he thought. Then he'd turned to Francine, removed his hat and leaned forward and kissed her.

His timing couldn't have been worse.

She'd turned away as he was making his move.

The result was that he smacked her on the ear with his lips, which startled Francine so that she let out a squeal. Then what looked like twin boys popped up in front of his buggy and began making smooching sounds.

Francine had screamed at the boys in such a way that it had surprised Noah. After all, they were only boys being boys. Then she had started to cry, and he hadn't known what to do so he'd patted her shoulder and said, "There, there."

He'd never heard those words from someone under sixty. He couldn't believe they came out of his mouth.

Francine had scrubbed at her eyes, proclaimed, "I hate it here," and jumped out of the buggy.

He didn't know what had caused her to run off.

His kiss?

The boys?

His ineffectual attempt to comfort her?

Dating was simply too hard.

And demeaning. It was definitely demeaning. He felt like a fish out of water. He felt like he had to be someone else, only he didn't know who that someone else was.

By the time he'd driven home, unhitched the buggy and pastured the horse, night had settled across the fields. For that he was glad. Maybe he wouldn't have to answer the fifty questions that had greeted him after his date with Jane.

But his father was sitting on the porch, rocking as he clamped a rarely lit pipe between his teeth.

Noah tried murmuring good-night and slipping by, but his father called him back. He motioned to the chair beside him and said, "Your *mamm* is glad you're back with us, Noah. We all are."

"And I'm glad to be back."

His *dat* rocked for a few minutes, struck a match and lit the pipe. Finally he said, "Do you think you'll stay?"

"*Ya.* I told you that. I'm done wandering."

"Because it would break your *mamm*'s heart for you to leave again. That's why she's so intent on finding you a *fraa*."

"I thought it was your idea."

His *dat* held the pipe by its bowl, pointed the end at him. "Wouldn't hurt you. Personally I think a man is happier when he's married with a family."

"I know you do."

"You don't?"

"I don't know. I used to. I used to be able to picture myself that way, but life seems to have different plans."

"Life doesn't have plans at all. 'For I know the thoughts that I think toward you, saith the Lord.'"

"Well, maybe the Lord's plan isn't for me to be married."

"Have you prayed on it?"

"I guess."

They sat in silence, his father drawing on the pipe. Noah stared out into the darkness. Fireflies darted back and forth, and he could hear an owl call out to its mate.

"You're not the first in our family to wander, you know."

"I'm not?"

"My *bruder* Josiah."

"You never speak of him."

"What is there to say? He wrote, at first. I was only seventeen when he left, and he was twenty-two."

"A long time ago."

"Indeed."

"Where did he go?"

Instead of answering that question directly, his *dat* said, "Josiah was never happy. If it was winter, he longed for summer. And in the summer, he couldn't wait for the snows to come. There was something restless about his spirit, about his attitude toward life."

"So he left?"

"He did. The first couple of years, he would come back every few months. Long enough to raise my parents' hopes that he was staying. But he never stayed. Last I heard from him, he was in Nova Scotia living with the Mennonites. That was over twenty years ago."

"Nova Scotia?" Noah tried to imagine that. "Is he still Amish?"

"Couldn't say. I suppose some part of him will always be."

"You've never told me this before."

"You didn't need to hear it before."

"And now I do?"

"I'm not sure, son."

Noah thought about that a moment. He had no doubt that his *dat* cared for him, that he always had. He did question whether he'd ever be able to live up to his parents' expectations. So instead of trying to explain how humiliating his most recent venture into dating had been, he said good-night and walked into the house.

Chapter Seven

Olivia Mae sat at the kitchen table, her Bible open in front of her, clutching a cup of hot tea. On the floor beside her sat the bags of thrift-store sweaters. She'd intended to frog at least one of them, but then a heavy exhaustion had claimed her and she'd found herself unable to do anything but clutch the tea and occasionally take a sip of it. Darkness had fallen outside the window.

She wondered about Noah and Francine. Had their date gone well? Why did that thought not fill her with as much happiness as she'd thought it would? She wanted to find Noah a wife. She couldn't do anything about her bleak situation, but she might be able to help his. She told herself that maybe that was her purpose in life—to find love for others.

Mammi walked into the room, hobbled over

to the stove and placed her fingertips against the teapot.

"Should still be hot," Olivia Mae said. "Want me to make you a cup?"

Mammi shook her head as she reached for the tin of tea bags and plopped one into a cup. She covered it with hot water, dunked it repeatedly and then dropped the tea bag into the trash. Finally she joined Olivia Mae at the table, her fingers interlaced around the cup, a smile on her face.

"We have much to be grateful for."

"I guess."

"You're worried about him."

"Of course I am."

"But he's home now, and he wasn't harmed. You did *gut*, Olivia Mae. You found him, and you brought him home."

Olivia Mae wasn't sure how to respond to that. When she'd found her grandfather, sitting with his back pressed to the neighbor's barn, unsure of where he was or why he was there, her heart had broken. It was past time that she stopped ignoring their situation and did something about it. If she didn't, someone else would. Their neighbor, Isaac, had looked terribly concerned when she'd stumbled out from behind the barn, guiding her bicycle with one arm and her grandfather with the other. "Isaac will speak to Lucas."

"Of course he won't. There's no reason—"

"There is a reason, *Mammi*." She raised her eyes and studied her grandmother. This was a *gut* evening. *Mammi* was in the present for now. Perhaps she could make her see how desperate their situation was becoming. "It's Lucas's job—every bishop's job—to look after the people in their community."

"We are fine."

"We're not fine."

Mammi had been staring into her tea, looking out the window at the darkness, even studying the ceiling, but now she met Olivia Mae's gaze. "He frightened you."

"*Ya*, he did. *Daddi* didn't know where he was. He didn't recognize Isaac at all."

"We've known him for years, since before we moved to this house."

"Isaac is a *gut* neighbor and a *gut* friend. He'll speak to Lucas."

"And what will Lucas do?" *Mammi*'s chin came up defiantly, and Olivia Mae almost laughed. Eighty-eight years old and still stubborn.

"Lucas will come and speak with us. He'll want to know what he can do to help, and he'll insist that we take *Daddi* to the doctor."

"There's nothing the doctors can do. We both know that, and Lucas does, too."

"Maybe. Or maybe there are new medicines." But *Mammi* wasn't listening.

"I wish you could have known your *daddi* when he was younger. I first met Abe when he'd come down to help his parents with the harvest. Have I told you this before?"

Olivia Mae nodded slightly, but she didn't mind hearing the story again. There was grace and mercy and hope in the telling.

"He'd moved to Maine, where your *bruders* are now. I suppose they heard the way he bragged about the land there, heard his memories of a different time and took them to heart." *Mammi* sipped the tea, smiled slightly. "Abe was a hard worker, always was. When I first saw him he was covered in dirt, sweaty and he smelled bad. But I lost my heart the first time he smiled at me."

Olivia Mae was listening to *Mammi*, but instead of imagining her grandfather, her mind drifted to Noah, standing on their front porch and handing her the letter box, smiling shyly... Yes, she could see how a girl could lose her heart over a single smile.

"He was so strong, and I knew... I was certain he would take care of me. I never..." Her voice wobbled. "I never imagined this."

"*Daddi* may have many years left, but we need help. This isn't the first time he has wandered off. What if he ended up on the main road? What if he accepted a ride with a stranger? How would we find him?" Her resolve hardened at that thought, and the look of fear on *Mammi*'s face. This was too much for her, too much for the both of them. Olivia Mae had thought she was doing the right thing by allowing them to stay in their home, to spend their final years in a place they loved and were familiar with, but now she wasn't so certain.

"I'll call Ben tomorrow."

"Tomorrow is Sunday. Your *bruder* won't be checking the phone shack."

"Then I'll call him on Monday. I'll call him and tell him how things are. Maybe he will think of something that we haven't."

Mammi nodded, but only slightly. They both knew that Ben would want them to sell the house and move to Maine. He'd mentioned it more than once, and he'd only agreed to let Olivia Mae move in with their grandparents as long as it remained a *healthy environment*. Those were his exact words, and the memory of them almost made Olivia Mae put her head down on the table and weep.

Mammi had been determined to stay in Goshen—to cling to their old life. Moving to Maine wasn't what she wanted. It wasn't what she'd envisioned all of those years ago.

Daddi didn't seem to know where they were, and there was at least that to be thankful for. As far as Olivia Mae knew, he'd be just as happy living somewhere else.

And Olivia Mae? She didn't know what she wanted. She only knew that she had somehow failed in her attempt to allow her grandparents to spend their final years in the community where they'd always lived.

She dreamed that she was still searching for *Daddi*, only in the dream she couldn't find him. The days and nights melded together in the way of dreams, and she wandered constantly, calling his name with *Mammi*'s pleas in her ears.

Find him, Olivia Mae. Please find him.

She woke more tired than when she'd first lain down.

When she walked into the kitchen, she found *Daddi* sitting at the table, smiling and talking about a wren that he'd seen at the feeder. *Mammi* stood at the stove, pretending that all was well.

The morning sped by in a blur of activity— preparing for church, harnessing the mare to the buggy, helping her grandparents make their way down the porch steps. May sunshine splashed across the road, and birds sang and the mare clopped merrily down the road, tossing her head occasionally. Olivia Mae realized there was much to be grateful for, even in these times of trouble.

Perhaps she was being overly dramatic. There would be sunny days in Maine, as well. Or maybe Ben would think of another solution. She was determined to speak to Lucas after the service, which was taking place at his house. She wanted a chance to explain things without her grandparents interrupting.

The service calmed her fears and strengthened her resolve. The first sermon was from the Old Testament—Genesis, Chapter 37. Ezra was preaching, and his voice was calm, confident, assuring. "*Gotte* provided for Joseph, even as he sat in the well that his brothers had thrown him in. *Gotte* hadn't forgotten Joseph, and he hasn't forgotten you."

Daniel King preached the second sermon. It was from the book of Acts, the twenty-fifth verse of the sixteenth chapter—the story of Paul and Silas in prison. Olivia Mae knew the passage well. She'd often marveled at the terrible things the apostles had endured. More than once, she'd read this particular passage and been inspired by the fact that Paul and Silas were singing hymns to God, even as they were shackled in a cell.

"We're shackled, too," Daniel said. "For sure and certain we are. Only our shackles are made of different things—our fears, our disbelief, even our past can shackle us. But *Gotte*, His eye isn't on our past, it's on our future."

If ever there was a service that spoke to Olivia Mae's heart, that calmed her troubled thoughts, this was it. After the final hymn and prayer, she helped in the serving line and decided she would eat later. Looking out across the tables that had been set up on the lawn, she saw that Lucas had finished eating and was speaking to a group of children. It was a perfect time to ask if he had a few minutes to talk. She was walking toward him, when the shouting started behind her.

She turned toward the voices and was shocked to see Noah and Francine nose-to-nose.

Everyone was staring as she hurried over to them, though no one had interrupted the argument yet. It wasn't unheard of to have a disagreement at an Amish gathering, though it was rare at a church meeting. Most people were on their best behavior at church, but the Amish were as human as everyone else. Apparently either Francine or Noah had reached the limit of their patience.

"A horse blanket, Noah. I'm still itching."

"I'm sorry that I'm not fancy enough for you."

"Fancy? We didn't even have silverware."

"What does that—"

"You didn't even ask me what I would have liked to eat, or where I would have liked to go."

Jane was tugging on Francine's arms. Olivia Mae expected to find her friend in tears, but that wasn't the case at all. Francine was angry, and she was bound and determined that Noah know it.

Olivia Mae put a hand on Noah's arm. "Let's go for a walk."

He jerked away his arm, his attention still on Francine, on defending himself. "You didn't even try the food."

"I couldn't!" Francine turned and stomped toward the barn, Jane jogging to keep up.

Noah finally seemed to realize that they'd caused quite a scene. "Women," he muttered, and strode off in the opposite direction—toward the horse pasture.

Olivia Mae stood there, unsure whether to go after Francine or Noah.

"Want me to talk to him?" Noah's brother Justin was trying to hide a smile as he spoke to Olivia Mae.

"You think this is funny?"

"I think it's typical."

"Of?"

"A man who's on unfamiliar ground."

Which made a certain amount of sense. "I'll talk to him."

She hadn't had time to find out how the date went the night before, but from what she'd just seen, it had been a disaster. Why was she not surprised?

By the time she reached Noah, he was sitting with his back against a tree, studying the horses cropping at the new May grass.

She sat down beside him and waited.

Finally he said, "I told you I wasn't any good at this."

"You might have mentioned as much once or twice."

He turned to her, and she thought that Noah would proceed to defend himself. Instead he shook his head, smiled sadly and said, "You certainly do say what you think."

"As do you, from what I heard back there."

Noah tore off his hat, as if he needed something to stare at, something to do with his hands. He twirled it round and round, pausing now and then to dust off some imaginary dirt. Finally he said, "I thought I was doing what you said."

"Such as?"

"Well, I thought a picnic would be nice. You know, instead of a gas-station date."

"What's wrong with a restaurant?"

"I don't know. Too many people watching

you. You're trapped at a table with nothing to look at but each other. It's all very awkward."

"A picnic, it sounds good in novels..."

"Don't read many of those."

"But in reality a lot can go wrong."

"So I learned."

"Why don't you start from the beginning?"

He went through it all—how he'd arrived early, the food that he'd picked up, even the horse blanket and the kiss.

"Oh, my," she said, when he was finished.

"Ya." He smiled at her ruefully, like a schoolboy caught skipping class.

Telling the story seemed to have eased some of his tension. At least he was able to laugh at himself now. He stuck the hat back on his head and smiled at her. "So..."

"What?"

"Tell me what I did wrong."

"Are you sure you're ready to hear that?"

"You're the dating expert."

"Matchmaker—it's not the same thing."

"Whatever."

"All right. Well, as I said, a picnic is a chancy thing, especially for a first date."

"I should have stuck to a restaurant."

"Definitely. Then you don't have to worry about the food. You know it will be good, and your date can choose whatever she wants, which for Francine is very important."

"I don't understand."

Olivia Mae sighed, stared out at the horses and finally said, "Francine is diabetic."

Dawning spread across Noah's face. "All I had to drink was sodas."

"Plus fried chicken, potato chips and cookies—none of those things are good for a diabetic, and combined they probably would have sent her blood-sugar levels sky-high."

Noah sat forward and studied her. "I'm an idiot."

"*Nein.* You couldn't have known, but that's an important component of dating—you learn about the other person. For a fourth or fifth date, a picnic might be nice. But for a first date?"

"Chancy."

"*Ya.* I think Francine would have told you about her condition…eventually. She doesn't hide it exactly, and most of us know." Though as she thought about it, that alone didn't seem to explain the angry reaction that she'd seen from Francine earlier. "Was the park busy?"

"*Ya.* Kids everywhere."

"Oh."

"*Oh* what?"

"I'm sure she'd tell you herself if she was speaking to you, but Francine moved in with her *bruder* not so long ago, and she's been a little overwhelmed by the sheer number of children he has."

"She was probably hoping for an evening away from *kinder*."

"Probably. And then the kiss...to have it interrupted by two of her nephews, that was just a fine icing of embarrassment on top of an already overcooked cake."

Noah flopped back on the ground, staring up at the white wisps of clouds that were scudding across the sky. "Dating is so complicated."

"People are complicated, Noah. Whether you're dating or working on a business deal or being a *gut* neighbor. Every single person you meet is dealing with something."

He rolled over on his side, propped himself up on his elbow and asked, "How did you get so wise?"

"Never said I was."

"I'm being serious. Don't look at me like that. I really am. How did you learn to navigate so seamlessly through these kind of interactions, and why aren't you married?"

Olivia Mae thought her eyes were going to pop out of her head. "Did you really just ask me that?"

"I did."

"A little intrusive."

"Meaning you don't want to answer?"

"Meaning it's none of your business."

"Fair enough, though it's like asking a horse salesman why he doesn't own a horse."

Which was so ridiculous that it eased the knot of defensiveness in her stomach. "My family situation is…unique."

"You mean with your grandparents?"

She nodded instead of answering and looked back toward the picnic area. She'd intended to speak to Lucas about *Daddi*.

"I've got it." Noah sat up and resettled his hat, looking quite pleased with himself.

"Got what?"

"The solution."

"To?"

"My dating disasters."

"Oh, that's *gut* to hear."

He leaned forward, close enough that she could smell the shampoo he'd used that morning. Close enough that she wanted to scoot back to calm her racing heart.

"You need to teach me."

"Pardon me?"

"You need to give me dating lessons."

"What do you mean?"

"You and me. We'll go on a few dates…say, three. That would be a *gut* number. You can learn how to do most things if you do it three times."

"That's a ridiculous suggestion."

"Why? I learn better from doing."

"Do you?"

"I've already learned not to take a girl to a gas station or a picnic, but who knows how many more dating traps are waiting for me to stumble into them."

"So this would be…a learning experience."

"It's a perfect solution." He studied her closely, and then reached forward and tugged on her *kapp* string, something no one had done to her since she'd been a young teen in school with a crush on a boy.

"I can tell by the shock on your face and the way you're twirling that *kapp* string that I've made you uncomfortable. It's a *gut* idea, though. We'd keep it businesslike—nothing personal."

Olivia Mae had no idea why the thought of sitting through three dates with Noah Graber made her stomach twirl like she'd been on a merry-go-round. Maybe she was catching a stomach bug.

"Wait a minute. Are you trying to get out of your third date? Because you promised your *mamm* that you would give this thing three solid attempts."

"And I'll keep my word on that," Noah assured her. "After you've tutored me, you can throw some other poor unsuspecting girl my way."

Olivia Mae saw Lucas walking away from the group. He was alone. She'd rather stay here talking to Noah, but now was her chance. She stood, brushed off the back of her dress and pointed a finger at Noah, who still sat in the grass as if he didn't have a care in the world.

"All right. I'll do it, on one condition."

Noah rolled his eyes, but motioned for her to continue.

"You go find Francine and apologize to her."

"I would have done that anyway. I'm not an ogre, just a bit clueless."

"You said it, not me."

Chapter Eight

Noah was cautiously optimistic when he checked the phone shack on Monday, felt a bit more cynical on Tuesday and grew positively aggravated by Wednesday. He wasn't asking Olivia Mae to marry him. He was asking for some in-person tutoring. Obviously he'd missed the lesson on how to act like a gentleman—according to Francine, who put it in those exact words. Where did men learn what women expected from them? It certainly hadn't been taught in his one-room schoolhouse.

Perhaps Olivia Mae was having second thoughts.

Why did it even matter to him?

So what if she had given up on him?

Maybe she'd found a more important match to make.

Good riddance. He could get on with his life—finally.

Or so he told himself as he clomped into the phone shack after work on Wednesday. He usually took the bus into work since Shipshe was eleven miles away—a bit of a long ride in a horse and buggy. At breakfast, his *dat* had asked him to drive the buggy and pick up a plow part on his way home. The sky was dark and broody, which matched his thoughts perfectly. He'd simply explain to his mother that no one was willing to give him a chance, so she'd understand that he was unmatchable and he'd be able to start looking for a bachelor pad.

He didn't want to live with his parents forever, but he wasn't quite sure what his new place would look like.

Obviously he needed a place for his horse and buggy. Something with a small sheep pen might be good.

He didn't need a sheep pen!

He didn't even particularly like sheep.

Maybe someone had a *grossdaddi haus* they'd rent to him. Amish might live simply, but they were usually on the lookout for ways to supplement the family income. He was making enough at the auction house that he could afford to pay a modest rent.

He stepped into the phone shack and saw the

light blinking on the answering machine beside the flashing number 1. Probably it was a message for Widow King again. For an elderly woman with a large family spread out in Goshen who probably visited her once a week, she certainly did get a lot of phone messages. He picked up the pen and prepared to take down the name and number.

Instead he heard Olivia Mae's voice on the recorder. At the sound of her voice he felt a lightness in his chest as if a heavy burden had been lifted.

"This message is for Noah Graber. We could have your first lesson on Wednesday at five thirty if that's agreeable. No need to bring anything."

Five thirty? He glanced at his watch and confirmed that he had exactly fifteen minutes to get to Olivia Mae's. He wouldn't have time to go home and change. He wouldn't even have time to warn his *mamm* that he wouldn't be home for dinner, but then that tended to happen a couple of times a week and he knew she wouldn't worry. Sometimes auction work ran late. She'd taken to leaving him a plate in the oven, covered with a pan lid, the temperature turned to low.

Which left him no good excuse to refuse Olivia Mae.

Why would he refuse her? This was what he'd asked for.

But suddenly he wasn't so sure. His mouth went dry, and he wondered if he'd made his predicament even worse than it had been.

He stomped back out of the phone shack as the rain began pelting the pavement. Great. Now his horse would wait in the rain while he learned which fork to eat with. His mood mirrored the stormy sky above him as he climbed into the buggy and called out to Snickers.

Twenty-five minutes later, he pulled into Olivia Mae's lane, his attitude actually worse than it had been when he'd received the message. The door to the barn was open, so he directed the horse inside. Olivia Mae had left an old towel to wipe off the mare, as well as a bucket filled with water and another that he could scoop oats into. After taking care of Snickers's immediate needs, he dashed across to the front porch, thoroughly drenched by the time he ran up the steps.

Olivia Mae was standing by the front door. He skidded to a stop a few feet in front of her, his throat suddenly dry. He was unable to figure out whether to cross his arms or leave them at his side. If she noticed his awkwardness, she didn't comment on it. Instead she smiled, her brown eyes reminding him of a cup of rich, delicious warm cocoa.

She offered him a towel.

"What's this for?"

"To dry off with."

"Oh, yeah." He accepted the towel, but simply stared at it. Turning, he scowled at the table she'd set up in the middle of the porch. "We're eating out here?"

"Ya."

"It's pouring."

"I can see that."

"You wouldn't rather go inside?"

"Nein. Here is *gut.* I've moved everything back so we won't get wet."

"More wet."

"Right. So you won't get *more* wet."

He grumbled a reply. Was she so embarrassed of him that he couldn't even go inside the house? He towel-dried his hair, took off his jacket, put it over the back of the chair and plopped down. "Fine."

"Let's try that again."

"Excuse me?" If he wasn't imagining it, she was actually trying to hold back laughter.

"You're here for a lesson, Noah. Remember?"

"How could I forget?"

"Well, sometimes dates are going to start off badly, like this."

"You mean because I'm soaking wet, and I had to rush to get here since I only heard your message half an hour ago? Or because I'm tired, I'm hungry and we're eating on the porch in a rainstorm?"

"See, that's exactly what I mean."

"What?"

"You're grumpy—out of sorts."

"I'm grumpy?" He nearly touched the top of his head to see if steam was coming out of it.

"Now, I don't intend to have you walk back to the barn—"

"Thank goodness for small favors."

"Let's just start when you were coming up the stairs."

"Fine. Do I need to put my coat back on?"

She waved away his suggestion and tugged on his arm. Her small hand on him caused him to break out in a sweat, even though the day had turned cooler with the rain. So why was he sweating? Why did he suddenly feel seventeen again?

"Stand over here, as if you're just arriving. Only this time try not to scowl at me."

"I'm scowling?"

"Maybe say hello and ask how my day has been."

He thought of walking away then. "This is a bad idea. This entire evening is a bad idea."

"I thought you wanted to learn." Now her voice was serious, and the look on her face seemed to dare him to find a reason to back out of his commitment.

That was it. She expected him to turn tail and run.

Well, he'd just see about that.

He could withstand one dinner in the rain. In fact, now that he could smell the food, his stomach had begun to growl. It would be foolish to leave before he had a chance to eat. So he stood straighter, walked back to the edge of the porch, where a spattering of rain still hit his back, and said, "Olivia, may I step forward three steps?"

"Now you're making fun of me and my name."

"Am not."

"Are too. You know my name is Olivia *Mae*, and you're playing on the word *may...*" She closed her eyes and pulled in a deep breath.

Ha! Mission accomplished. He was getting to her. He was testing her patience in the same way that she tried his. Two could play at that game.

"Try again, please."

"All right. Olivia Mae, you look beautiful tonight. How was your day?"

"It was *gut*. Nice rain we're having."

"Nice indeed."

She motioned toward the chair where he'd been sitting a few minutes earlier. "I thought we'd have a picnic outside, but since it's raining I moved it to the porch."

"*Gut* idea."

He started to sit, but when she shook her head, he froze.

"Problem?" he asked in a stage whisper.

"Pull out my chair for me. It's the gentlemanly thing to do."

"So now we're teaching me to be a gentleman?"

"It's a goal, *ya*."

He was still put out with her, but found it impossible to stay angry. Something about that impish grin she wore stole his irritation and sent it out into the storm.

"May I help you with your chair, Olivia Mae?"

She rolled her eyes, but allowed him to pull back the chair and then scoot it in.

"I've never seen my *dat* do that for my *mamm*."

"It would be awkward to do so the rest of your married life."

"It's our first date. We've already decided we're getting married?" He was enjoying teasing her, but Olivia Mae was all seriousness. He'd have thought she was a schoolmarm teaching advanced math.

"Many of the things you do on early dates are to set the tone of a relationship. Once that relationship, that bond, is established, some things are no longer necessary." She stared up at the corner of the porch ceiling as if she was trying to remember something, then added, "Though it's always kind to open a buggy door for a woman no matter how long you've been married."

"I thought today's women wanted more independence." The teasing had slipped away, replaced by his general confusion with the opposite gender.

"Women are not a deep dark secret, Noah. At the heart of it all, women want the same thing that men do—to be respected." She straightened the fork, which was positioned just so beside her plate. "As far as independence, well, I couldn't answer that."

The next few moments passed in an agonizing fashion.

He felt like a *youngie*.

She reminded him to put his napkin in his lap.

She told him to pick up the dishes and offer them to her first, then serve himself.

"Should I stand up and serve you?"

"You're kidding, but no, you shouldn't. You offer the dish to the woman first because she cooked the meal and you want her to have the first selection."

"Seems like my *mamm* always serves herself last."

"That's exactly my point. So take this plate of chicken, for instance. A woman might stand in a hot kitchen, frying chicken over spattering grease, and by the time the plate goes around the table, there's little left for her to eat but a wing."

"Maybe she needs to cook more." He smiled to show he wasn't serious. He passed her the mashed potatoes, hot rolls and salad. Both of their plates were now quite full, but she still hadn't picked up a fork, and his stomach was growling.

"My family usually prays silently. Does yours?"

"Ya."

"All right. So once the food is served, simply bow your head. Your date will do the same."

He bowed his head but peeked at her.

"Don't do that."

"Yes, ma'am."

"Pray as you usually would and then a soft *amen* will indicate you're finished but not interrupt your date if she's still praying."

"Can I start eating now?"

"Nein. Wait for her to look up at you." She raised her head and smiled at him, and another piece of the ice that had formed around his heart melted away.

Olivia Mae did not like the way her pulse beat faster when Noah gave her that beseeching look. This was a lesson, nothing more. He'd said absolutely nothing to indicate he might be interested in her romantically. If anything, he'd made it rather obvious that he still didn't think she could find a match for him.

While she corrected his manners, which were as bad as any bachelor's but no worse than some she'd worked with, she tried to remain detached and professional. It was hard, given what was going on in her personal life. Her thoughts drifted to the phone conversation with her brother and the doctor appointments for her grandparents.

"Where did you go?" Noah asked.

"Go?"

"I lost you there for a minute."

"I'm sorry. It's been a difficult week."

Noah cocked his head and waited. She'd noticed that he was good at listening once he conquered his initial battle of nervousness. But this evening wasn't about her or her problems. It was about Noah and helping him to prepare for his next real date.

"Tell me one of your silly jokes."

"Really?"

"Sure. Make me laugh. I could use a laugh today." She said it in a lighthearted way, but even she heard the pain beneath her words.

Noah sat back and rubbed his chin as if he needed to think long and hard, but he couldn't keep up the act for long. He pushed his plate forward—a plate that looked as if it had been licked clean—and crossed his arms on the table.

"What do you get if you cross an angry sheep and a moody cow?"

"A sheep with mad cow disease?"

"Moody, not mad. That was a *gut* answer, though."

"Okay, tell me. What do you get if you cross an angry sheep and a moody cow?"

"An animal that's in a ba-a-a-a-aad moo-oo-ood."

He sounded exactly like a sheep and then like a cow—or enough like one to make her laugh. "Your imitation is better than your joke."

"I'll take that as a compliment."

He smiled and seemed to relax for the first time since he'd arrived, causing Olivia Mae to realize he was quite a handsome man. He had nice hair, and a strong profile and beautiful eyes. She'd barely processed those thoughts, when her *mammi* pushed through the screen door.

"Elizabeth. What are you doing out here in the rain?"

Olivia Mae jumped up. "I'll be right back."

"Can I help?" Noah called after her, but she was already at the door, guiding *Mammi* back inside.

"I couldn't find you," *Mammi* said.

"I told you I was on the porch, remember? Giving Noah a lesson."

"Looked to me like you were giving him dinner." *Mammi*'s hands shook slightly as Olivia Mae led her back into the kitchen, stepping around the soup pot and basin that she'd placed under the leaks in the roof. The rain made a *pat-pat-pat* sound as it plopped into the containers.

"I don't know any boy named Noah. Where is Henry?"

Olivia's heart sank at the mention of her father's name. She'd hoped that when her grandmother called her Elizabeth it had been a slip, but it seemed that she was experiencing another one of her episodes that threw her into the past.

"Let me fix you some hot tea."

"*Ya*, all right. Then you can go back out to Henry, though I don't know why you're eating on the porch."

"It's a picnic, *Mammi*."

"In the rain?"

"Well, that I didn't plan on."

While the water in the kettle heated up, Olivia Mae checked in on *Daddi*. He was sitting in his favorite chair in the living room, oblivious to the rain splattering into a bowl next to his chair, trying to make sense of some article in the *Budget*.

At least he didn't appear agitated. She pulled a knitted throw from the basket in the corner of the room and placed it across his lap, righted the paper, which he was trying to read upside down, and kissed him on top of the head.

The kettle had begun to whistle when Noah rapped lightly on the screen door.

"Everything all right in there?" He'd cupped his hands around his eyes and was peering inside.

"Fine. It's all fine." She rushed to the door and pushed it open, forcing him back. "I just needed to help my grandparents."

"Did she call you Elizabeth?"

"I'll be out with dessert in just a minute. Just, um, take a seat and I'll be right back with some cake." Before he could ask any more questions that she'd have to ignore, she fled inside.

Daddi had turned the paper upside down again and was growing increasingly frustrated with it. She needed to get it out of his hands before he had a complete meltdown.

Her *mammi* called out from the kitchen, "Elizabeth, the kettle is ready... I'll just make us some tea."

Olivia Mae didn't think *Mammi* was steady

enough on her feet for tea making. She hurried back toward the kitchen and tripped over the soup pot, sending it sloshing across the floor. Dashing to retrieve it, she slipped on the wet floor, grabbed for the doorjamb and fell, landing hard on her backside. She sat there on the floor—wet, frustrated and unsure whether to run to her *daddi* or *mammi*—when a scream came from the kitchen.

She attempted to stand up, but the floor had become as slippery as an ice rink. Suddenly she felt two strong hands lifting her to her feet.

"Check on your *mammi*." Noah's voice was low, calm and steady. "I'll go and sit with your *daddi* for a minute."

Before she could answer, he'd retrieved the soup bowl, placed it under the biggest leak and hurried back toward the living room. Olivia Mae rushed into the kitchen to find the kettle on the floor and *Mammi* standing with a hot pad in her left hand, glancing around wildly.

"Elizabeth. Thank goodness you're here. I don't know what made me drop that kettle. It was as hot as a live coal."

"I'll take care of it, *Mammi*." Her grandmother was right-handed. Apparently she'd remembered to pick up a hot pad, but had put it in the wrong hand. "Let me help you to the table. Did you burn yourself?"

"*Nein*, I don't think so."

"Let me see." Olivia Mae sat in the chair next to her and pulled her grandmother's hand into her lap. The palm was a bright red, but it didn't look as if it would blister. She breathed a silent prayer of gratitude and smiled at *Mammi*. "We should put your hand in water."

"Seems to be plenty of that around here." *Mammi* glanced around the room, then met Olivia Mae's eyes. They both started laughing at the same time.

Perhaps it was relief over the fact that *Mammi* hadn't been burned more badly than she was. Maybe it was the look on Noah's face as he'd helped her up from the floor, or it could be that exhaustion had finally taken its toll. Whatever the reason, tears rolled down Olivia Mae's face. *Mammi* reached forward and thumbed them away. "You're a *gut doschder*."

"*Danki*."

She didn't bother to correct her grandmother, to explain that she was her granddaughter, not her daughter. Instead she snatched a bowl out of the drainer that sat next to the sink, stuck it under the nearest leak and brought the bowl filled with rainwater to the table. Gently she placed *Mammi*'s hand in it.

"Does it hurt?"

"*Nein*. It was a silly thing to do." She glanced

down at the hot pad she still clutched in her other hand. "For some reason, I had it in my left and I always use my right. Getting old and forgetful, I guess."

Rather than agreeing or disagreeing with her, Olivia Mae patted her arm and made sure her hand stayed in the bowl of water. "I'm going to check on—" she almost said *Noah*, but at the last minute changed it "—*Daddi*. I'll be back in just a minute. Promise to stay put?"

"*Ya*. But you should pick up our kettle off the floor."

Olivia Mae accepted the hot pad, scooped up the kettle, placed it back on the stove and hurried into the living room. What she saw there stopped her in her tracks. Noah and *Daddi* were sitting at the small table near the window. Noah had moved it so it no longer sat under one of the leaks in their roof, and he and *Daddi* were engrossed in a game of checkers.

"Ha. Crown me," *Daddi* said.

"Got me again." Noah glanced up and smiled at her as she walked into the room.

Olivia Mae felt a surge of gratitude in that moment that threatened to overwhelm her. She'd put Noah through what must have been a difficult lesson on the front porch. She fully realized that no one liked being corrected and change— well, change was always difficult. Yet, here he sat, playing checkers with her *daddi* as if he had nothing better to do.

She skirted around yet another bowl and stopped beside the table. "How are we doing in here?"

"Gut." Daddi laughed. "Your beau isn't very *gut* at checkers."

She was about to correct him when Noah said, "Does that mean you're afraid to play me again?"

"I thought you'd be begging for mercy." *Daddi* proceeded to reset the checkerboard, his hands shaking only slightly and a smile playing across his lips. All the frustration from a few moments earlier had been forgotten, and he seemed to not have noticed the minor emergency in the kitchen.

Noah jumped up from the chair and pulled Olivia Mae a few feet away. Lowering his voice, he said, "We're doing fine here, but how is your *mammi*?"

"Okay. Only a little burn."

"Does she need to see a doctor?"

"Nein. I have her soaking her hand in water. I'd like to put some aloe vera on it. Could you stay with *Daddi* just a while longer?"

"Are you kidding? I couldn't bear to miss another thrashing at the checkerboard." He touched her arm as she turned away, and that—

the simple act of him placing his hand on her arm—nearly caused the tears to spill over again. For some reason Noah's kindness cut her to her core, and that made no sense at all. Had it been so long since she'd accepted help from someone?

The next hour seemed unreal, as if it was happening to someone else. She cut two leaves from the aloe vera plant in the windowsill, washed them in the sink, then sliced them open and placed the jelly inside of each stem against her grandmother's palm.

"Does that feel all right?"

"Ya." Mammi reached forward and cupped the side of Olivia Mae's face. *"Danki*, Olivia Mae."

Her grandmother calling her by the correct name righted her world and eased the last of the tension in her shoulders. They were okay. They'd made it through another event. She had no idea what brought on her *mammi*'s episodes, but since Lucas had insisted that she take them to the doctor, she might know more by the end of the week. For now, it was enough that her grandmother was back in the present.

"It must be hard, living with old folks like us."

"Not hard at all."

"Daddi is okay?"

"He's fine—playing checkers with Noah."

"There's some apple crumb cake left. Maybe we could have that with some hot tea."

"Cake and tea sounds *gut*."

They spent the next half hour all gathered around the kitchen table, enjoying the cake and the tea and one another's company.

The storm had moved on and the sky was clearing by the time she walked Noah out to the barn. "*Danki*, for your help."

But she could tell, even in the last of the summer evening's light, that he wasn't going to let her off the hook so easily. Instead of climbing up into his buggy, he sat down on a bale of hay near the barn door and patted the place beside him.

"Sit. Talk to me."

"About what?" she asked lightly.

"Talk to me, Olivia Mae."

Her shoulders sagged and she dropped down onto the bale of hay next to him. "You're here for a lesson, and I'm sorry it was interrupted."

"I'm not."

"What do you mean?"

"I mean, this is your life, and I'm not sorry I had a glimpse of it. But tell me what's going on. Obviously you're struggling."

The old defensiveness reared its head, and it

took all of her control to stay put. "I don't know what you mean."

"You don't?" He shifted on the bale of hay so that he could study her. "Your grandmother called you by the wrong name, then burned herself because she couldn't properly pick up a kettle. Your grandfather was nearly in a state of panic sitting in the living room by himself, and if I'm not mistaken he thinks Eisenhower is still president. Lastly, your home's roof has more holes than a sieve."

"I was hoping you wouldn't notice."

"Which part?"

"All of it?" Olivia Mae sat forward and buried her face in her hands. Why was this so humiliating? Why was it so difficult to admit how desperate their situation was?

Noah was embarrassed. He'd actually thought he had problems, but he understood now that his were minor compared to Olivia Mae's. His biggest problem at the moment was whether he would continue living with his parents or strike out on his own. He'd had no idea that Olivia Mae was dealing with such a volatile situation. He hadn't taken the time to know, but he would now—that's what good friends did, they listened.

"No rush," he assured her. "Snickers seems quite content here in your barn."

"Don't you have somewhere you need to be?" She lowered her hands and smoothed out her apron.

"Me? *Nein.* I had a dating lesson tonight that went much better than I expected."

"It did go well. Didn't it?"

"No changing the subject. Maybe start with the roof. Why haven't you had it fixed?"

"No money? It seemed easier to hope it wouldn't rain? I wasn't sure who to ask?"

"The first two might be true, but not the last. If you'd told the bishop, he would have had a work crew out here before the end of the week."

"You're right. I know that—yes, but *Daddi* was in the hospital."

"When?"

"Before you were here, and the total of what we owed for doctors and the hospital was quite high. The benevolence fund paid his bill. I wasn't ready to ask for more help."

"Okay. We'll come back to that. What's going on with Abe? Does he have Alzheimer's?"

Olivia Mae flinched at the word. She and her grandmother hadn't discussed it, as if not saying the name of the disease could keep it at bay.

"I think so."

She told Noah how *Daddi* often had trouble dressing correctly, that he sometimes couldn't remember the names of common household items and other times he did things like put his reading glasses in the icebox. She told him about her grandfather wandering off the previous Saturday.

Noah could tell by the way that she wrapped her arms around her middle how terrified she was.

"It's what you were speaking to Lucas about on Sunday, *ya*?"

"*Ya*. After *Daddi* wandered off, I searched and called and prayed and searched some more. Then when I found him, he didn't recognize me, didn't know where he was. Worse, he was so frightened that it broke my heart."

"I can't imagine what that must have been like for you."

"It was a wake-up call, that's what it was. I knew then that I had to speak with Lucas. I had to come clean about all of this—though I didn't mention the roof. I planned to after we worked out the more immediate stuff."

"Such as?"

"Lucas insisted that I take them both into the doctor. We have appointments tomorrow."

"For Rachel and Abe?"

"*Ya*. *Mammi* doesn't have whatever *Daddi* has, but there's something wrong. I don't know what it is."

She stared down at her hands, and he forced

himself not to rush her. From the way she was acting, he was the first person she'd talked to about this—other than the bishop.

Did that make them friends?

More than friends?

Finally she glanced up and admitted, "I don't know what to do anymore, so I called my *bruders*."

"They live in Maine?"

"Uh-huh. I told Ben everything. I'm supposed to call him back after we see the doctor, but regardless what we learn tomorrow, I know his answer."

"Which is?"

"That we move to Maine."

Noah felt a jolt of surprise for the first time since she'd begun baring her soul. "Do you want to move to Maine?"

"Nein." Now she jumped up and began pacing in the doorway to the barn. "I do not, and I don't think it would be *gut* for them, either. I think they should be here, where they've always lived. Goshen is where they met and married. It's where things are familiar, and we have a church community that we know."

She stared across the yard at the house.

He could tell that she was exhausted and a little lost.

What she'd just described was a lot for a

young woman to carry on her own, and the fact that she and Abe and Rachel had made it this long was testament to how strong she was.

Noah stood and moved behind her. He wanted to put his arms around her, but he didn't. He had the sense that she was like a newborn fawn—easily frightened and apt to dart away. When she turned to look at him, he couldn't help smiling.

"What?"

"Only that you look pretty standing there, rain still dripping off the leaves and the last of the sun's light pushing across the field."

She didn't respond, but her cheeks blushed a pretty rose color. He felt an irresistible urge to pull her into his arms and kiss her. Something told him he wouldn't make a mess of it this time, not like he had when he'd tried to kiss Francine outside her brother's house. He realized that had been foolish. He hadn't done it because he'd cared about Francine, but because he'd been curious, nothing more.

He almost asked, "Olivia, may I...?" but then Snickers neighed, and Olivia Mae plastered on a smile, and the moment slipped away.

"You should go. Your horse is growing impatient."

"And you need to get back inside with your grandparents."

She nodded in agreement, watched as he

backed Snickers out of the barn and stood beside him as he climbed up into the buggy.

"I can't fix the situation with your grandparents, though I'll pray that tomorrow goes well."

"Danki."

"But I can fix your roof."

She'd been standing close to the buggy door, but now she drew back and crossed her arms. "There's no need—"

"To fix your roof? *Ya.* There is." Then, realizing that she might be worried he'd do a bad job, he added, "I did some roofing while I was in New York. Pretty sure my *dat* has some leftover supplies from when he redid our roof a couple of years ago. It's no problem."

"But...the storm is passed."

"Bound to be another. There always is. If it's okay. I'll come over after I do my chores in the morning."

"No auction?"

"Actually, it's my day off."

"Which you usually spend working at your parents' place. And don't bother denying it because you told me as much while we were eating."

"My parents would insist that I come over and help, and I don't mind, Olivia Mae. In fact, I'm happy to do it." He realized as he drove away that it was true—he was happy at the thought of easing her burden a bit.

But that part about her moving to Maine left him with a new kind of knot in his stomach.

Chapter Nine

Their doctor's appointment the next day was for three in the afternoon. Olivia Mae spent the morning baking, cleaning and trying to convince *Daddi* that it wasn't cold enough to wear his winter coat outside.

Noah arrived around noon and was nearly done with the roof when they left at two. The image in her mind as she drove the buggy down the lane was of him on top of the roof—straw hat pulled low against the afternoon sun, sleeves rolled up to his forearms, his hair curling and damp from the sweat running down his face.

She didn't know what she'd done to deserve a friend like Noah Graber, but she was grateful that the Lord had seen fit to send him her way.

Lucas must have explained their situation to the doctor, because they'd only been waiting twenty minutes when Dr. Laney Burkhart called all three of them into her office. She was a middle-aged woman, with purple-framed glasses and shoulder-length red hair. She had a kindly expression and looked straight at them as she spoke. She didn't act in a hurry, which immediately put Olivia Mae at ease.

"Your bishop explained a little of your situation to me over the phone, but I wanted to speak with you as a family before I begin my examinations. Then we'll meet back here when I'm done."

Mammi clasped her purse and nodded.

Daddi had become preoccupied with an old-fashioned slide puzzle that had been sitting on the corner of the doctor's desk. His suspenders were twisted and his hair was sticking up in the back, but overall he seemed to be having a pretty good day.

Neither her grandmother nor grandfather said anything, which left it to Olivia Mae to speak up. "There have been some...issues for a while now."

"And you're the primary caregiver for your grandparents?"

"I live with them, *ya*. I help out where I can."

"Olivia Mae has been a huge blessing to us," *Mammi* chimed in. "Our grandsons, they wanted us to move to Maine, but Olivia Mae and I, we both think it's best for Abe to stay in a place that he's familiar with."

Dr. Burkhart attempted to have a conversation with *Daddi*, but he simply looked at *Mammi* each time the doctor asked him a question. Once he looked out the window and said, "I bet it's cold out there." Dr. Burkhart jotted down a few notes and paged through the forms they'd filled out while they'd waited to be called back to the office.

Finally she turned her attention back to Olivia Mae and *Mammi*. "Have you noticed any recent changes or deterioration in Mr. Lapp's condition?"

"He forgets things sometimes, but don't we all?" *Mammi* attempted to make a joke of the situation.

But Olivia Mae understood that it was time they come to terms with what they were dealing with. They were well past the point of glossing over the truth of their situation. "*Daddi* has wandered off several times. When we find him, he seems confused about where he is and also when."

"When?"

"Sometimes, he thinks it's the past or he thinks it's winter when it's summer. It's as if his thinking process is jumbled in some way."

Daddi glanced up, perhaps sensing that they

were talking about him. He seemed to notice the doctor for the first time. "Do I know you?"

"We just met, Mr. Lapp."

Daddi accepted that with the innocence of a child. He nodded, smiled and then leaned forward to confide in the doctor. "We're going for a treat after this—ice cream. I just love ice cream. Don't you?"

"I do," Dr. Burkhart said. "Strawberry is my favorite. What's yours?"

Instead of answering, *Daddi* glanced around the office and finally repeated, "We're going for a treat after this—ice cream."

The doctor nodded and continued with her questions. "Mrs. Lapp, how would you describe your health at this point?"

"Oh, I'm as fit as the buggy horse in the parking lot. Maybe not as strong as I once was."

The doctor allowed silence to permeate the room.

Olivia Mae cleared her throat and said, "Sometimes *Mammi* forgets who I am. Sometimes she calls me the wrong name."

"I do?"

Olivia Mae nodded, dying a thousand deaths at the look of confusion on her grandmother's face. "It doesn't last long, but sometimes she is confused. It's—it's different from whatever *Daddi* is dealing with. She might go for days without an episode, but then it comes on all a sudden with no warning that I can tell."

Dr. Burkhart scribbled a few additional notes, then as if on some secret signal, a nurse tapped lightly on the door and walked into the office.

"My nurse is going to get you both in a room," the doctor said. "Mr. and Mrs. Lapp, if you'll just follow Amy, I'll be with you in a moment."

Which left Olivia Mae alone in the office with the doctor.

She told her everything—her fears, *Daddi*'s growing confusion, *Mammi*'s unpredictability, their precarious living situation. By the time she was done, the doctor had pushed a box of tissues her way, and Olivia Mae was trying to dry her tears without making her eyes red and puffy.

"You've been dealing with a lot, but you did the right thing bringing them in today. Too many times, caregivers attempt to deal with a situation like this on their own. There are things that we can do to help—there are social services for the family, some new medications that might help your grandfather and support groups for you."

"I'm not sure how much of that they'd agree to."

"We're getting ahead of ourselves. I want you to go back out to the waiting room, make yourself a hot drink and try to lose yourself in one of the fabulous magazines on our coffee table. I think we even have the latest *People*, which, if I'm not mistaken, features Brad Pitt."

Olivia Mae wasn't interested in *People* or *Better Homes & Gardens* or even *National Geographic*. But the hot tea that she made from the Keurig machine did help to calm her stomach, and the thought of Noah—and Lucas and her brothers—praying for them calmed her fears.

By the time they all met back in Dr. Burkhart's office, she was ready to know what they were facing.

"You cannot escape the responsibility of tomorrow by evading it today," as Abraham Lincoln had said. She'd done a report on him in the fifth grade. She could still remember the tall black hat she'd made out of construction paper. She'd worn it as she read her report in front of the class. She remembered being so nervous that day and thinking that life as an adult would be much easier than life as a student. What she wouldn't give to go back and be young and carefree again—even for just one week.

Dr. Burkhart got right to the point.

"I want to caution you that I have only done a cursory exam today. My specialty is not geriatrics, though my colleagues and I see many older patients here in our offices. You might want to consult with a neurologist, a psychiatrist or a psychologist. I can give you referrals for any of those."

"But what do you think?" Olivia Mae asked. Already she felt comfortable with the doctor. She liked the way that the woman spoke to her grandparents, the way she waited for an answer and the amount of time that she was taking with them.

"I believe that Mr. Lapp is somewhere between stage four and five on the Alzheimer's scale."

"So he has it? You're sure?" *Mammi*'s eyes widened in fear.

Olivia Mae reached over and clasped her hand. As for *Daddi*, he'd once again taken to playing with the puzzle on the doctor's desk— sliding pieces left and then right, trying to create the picture of a boat.

"At this point, there's not a definitive test for Alzheimer's, but based on the things that you both have told me, as well as my exam of Mr. Lapp, I'd say that it's highly likely that he does have the disease."

Olivia Mae wasn't a bit surprised at what the doctor was saying. She'd known—probably for over a year now she'd known. She'd even gone to the library and used the computers to research the disease. She'd known what diagnosis the doctor would give them, but she hadn't wanted to face that truth.

These dear people were her responsibility, and there was no unhearing what the doctor had said. "Stage four and five. What does that mean?"

"Stage four is what we call mild and is characterized by decreased ability to manage complex activities of daily life—manage finances or prepare a meal."

"Abe never was a *gut* cook," *Mammi* murmured.

"Stage five is moderate—the inability to choose proper clothing, that sort of thing."

Olivia Mae and *Mammi* exchanged a knowing look. *Daddi* had insisted on wearing his winter coat and a wool cap when he'd dressed for the day. They'd only dissuaded him by bringing up the idea of ice cream as a treat afterward.

They spoke for the next ten minutes about what could be done to help *Daddi*'s situation, and the doctor gave them a folder with brochures and pamphlets in it. When Dr. Burkhart turned her attention to *Mammi*, she smiled and said, "I have somewhat better news for you."

Noah ran out of work to do on the roof an hour after Olivia Mae left with her grandparents. He could have gone home. He probably should have gone home. He'd told his brother that he'd try to get back in time to help him in the fields.

But he couldn't do that.

He needed to stay and talk to Olivia Mae.

So he packed the leftover supplies he hadn't used back into his buggy, and then he swept the front porch where his hammering had left piles of dust and debris. Satisfied it looked as clean as when he'd shared dinner there with Olivia Mae the night before, he went inside and picked up all the bowls scattered on the floor, shaking his head as he did so. Olivia Mae was one stubborn woman. She'd rather spread a half-dozen pots and bowls around the place than ask for help?

He knew the feeling, though.

It was more than embarrassment or pride; it was a sickening feeling that your problems were too big to admit to—certainly too big to ask help for. He'd felt that way personally for a long time. If he was honest with himself, he'd felt like a freak because he still wasn't married and everyone his age was. He'd convinced himself that there was something wrong with him and that such a future wasn't even possible.

But last night, his lesson with Olivia Mae had sent his thoughts veering off in different directions.

He'd actually enjoyed the time he'd spent with her, even playing checkers with her grandfather.

He'd thought about her a lot after he'd left.

And he found himself looking forward to their next *lesson.*

Not that he was getting emotionally involved with Olivia Mae Miller. He understood that she was out of his league, and besides that—she was probably moving to Maine soon.

He walked through the barn and noticed that the horse stall needed mucking out. After that, he checked on her sheep, though he knew nothing about the animals. He was just wondering if he should leave a note, when he heard the clip-clop of their old buggy horse coming down the lane.

Olivia Mae pulled up to the front porch and helped her grandparents out of the buggy.

"Go inside with them," Noah said, grabbing the reins of the horse.

"But Zeus needs—"

"I'll take care of the horse." He waited for her to nod in agreement, then he led the horse across the yard to the barn, unharnessed the gelding and set him out to pasture. By the time he was finished, Olivia Mae was walking toward him.

"Abe and Rachel doing okay?"

"*Ya.* They're resting. The afternoon was tiring for them."

He studied her a minute, wondering what he

should do, and finally it occurred to him to simply ask. "Should I go? Do you want to be alone, or..."

"You probably have things to do at home."

He shook his head and waited.

"Then I'd like you to stay, if you don't mind."

"I don't mind at all."

He wanted to reach for her hand, but she'd already turned away and was walking toward the sheep pen.

"I haven't formally introduced you to my sheep. This is Ashlee, Gabriela, Izso, Loren, Joann and Alicia." She touched each on the top of the head as they crowded around her.

Noah couldn't help grinning. "Is there going to be a quiz?"

"Could you pass one if there were?"

"Nope."

They both laughed, and all the tension and the worry about Olivia Mae and her grandparents and her home melted away. Everything was okay for this moment, and that was enough. Unfortunately, Noah's feelings of tranquility lasted about as long as a sheep's attention span, which was apparently remarkably short.

As they scattered back out into the pasture, chasing something he couldn't see, Olivia Mae said, "*Daddi* has Alzheimer's."

"They're sure?"

"As sure as they can be without dissecting his brain. I think—I think I've known for a long time."

"I'm sorry, Olivia Mae."

"It isn't your fault." But she didn't smile the way she usually did. Instead she began walking down the length of the fence. He hurried to follow her. She picked up a soccer ball and threw it toward the sheep. She stopped to upend what looked like a piece of playground equipment that had been turned over, and she finally plopped down on a stool that was inside the three-sided shelter at the far end of the pasture.

They had a good view of the house from there—the house and the sheep and the entire farm really. It wasn't very large.

"Did you know one year's growth of fleece equals about eight pounds of wool?"

Noah shook his head and sank to the ground beside her. The littlest of the sheep—was it Izso or Alicia?—ran over, stopped short and then proceeded to nudge up against Olivia Mae.

"Is that a lot of wool?"

"To me it is. When I first bought the sheep, I had these plans of spinning the wool into yarn and having a little shop of things I'd knitted. I even learned how to card and spin. I had this entire future planned out."

"You could still do that."

Olivia Mae shook her head, swiped at her tears and sat up straighter. "On the way back from the doctor's, we stopped by the phone shack, and I called my *bruder*. He took the news pretty well, but he says we need to move up there, where I can have more help."

"We can help you here."

"He says *Mammi* and *Daddi* need to be around their family—their *entire* family. He says it's more than I should have to handle on my own."

Noah didn't know how to answer that. He only knew that he felt like a rock had landed in the bottom of his stomach.

"And what do you think?"

Olivia Mae shrugged. "I told myself I was staying here in Goshen, here on their farm, for them."

She looked directly at him now, and the misery in her eyes tore at his heart.

"But maybe I wasn't. Maybe it was for me, because I didn't want to move, because I like Goshen more than Maine. Maybe I was being selfish all along."

"You don't strike me as a selfish person."

She let out a sigh, pushed the sheep gently out of her lap, stood and brushed off her dress. When she squared her shoulders, he knew that

Olivia Mae, Matchmaker and Caretaker Extraordinaire, was back.

"How long…?" Noah cleared his throat. "How long until you move?"

"*Gotte* knows."

"Yes, but do you have any idea?"

She laughed and started walking back toward the pasture gate, toward her responsibilities.

"Ben is going to put an ad in the next issue of the *Budget*. He thinks we have a *gut* chance of selling the place before fall. He thinks someone will be looking for greener pastures and snap it up even though it's small. You know how it is with *Plain folk…*" She emphasized the last two words and wiggled her eyebrows.

Unfortunately he understood that her bravado was merely a show. Underneath, he suspected her heart was breaking.

They'd reached his buggy when he remembered to ask about her grandmother.

"That wasn't the only news today. Dr. Burkhart thinks *Mammi* is having a reaction between her blood-pressure medicine and the statin she takes to lower her cholesterol. She's going to change one of them, and hopefully the bouts of forgetfulness will stop. She didn't think that *Mammi* has Alzheimer's."

"That is *gut*." Suddenly Noah had an overwhelming urge to do something, anything, to ease Olivia Mae's burdens. Fixing her roof wasn't enough. Members of their church should have done that long ago, and they would have— if they'd known.

"How about I take you out to eat tomorrow?"

"I don't think I can—"

"Leave them for a few minutes? I could ask my sister-in-law to come and sit with them."

"*Nein.* It's not that."

"What then?"

She'd been standing beside Snickers, running her hand up and down the mare's neck. Finally she turned to look at him, a twinkle in her eyes. "We're not dating, Noah. You don't have to take me out to eat."

"Oh, *ya.* Sure. I know that. But the thing is..." He stepped closer and lowered his voice as if he was sharing a secret. "I've heard that I'm pretty bad at restaurant dates, and I'm supposed to be learning from you because you're an expert and all."

She swatted his arm, blushed prettily and looked at him in a way that caused his heart to soar. "Okay, Romeo."

"Who's Romeo?"

"Romeo and Juliet. Shakespeare."

When he shook his head, she laughed and said, "Honestly. Did you pay attention at all in school?"

"I don't remember reading Shakespeare."

"Maybe we didn't. Maybe I checked that out from the library. Anyway, it was a compliment."

"In that case, *danki*." He climbed up into the buggy. "Pick you up at six?"

"Sure."

He was about to call out to the mare when she leaned in and said, "And *danki* for fixing the roof."

Her eyes met his, and he thought for a moment that she was going to kiss him, but instead she stepped away and waved as he pulled off down the lane.

Since Noah had missed out on helping his brother in the fields, he offered to muck out the horse stalls after dinner.

"You won't see me turning down that offer."

Which was a nice enough thing to offer to do, but once he was out there doing it, he wondered if he'd lost his mind. It seemed like he'd spent all day around manure—first in Olivia Mae's barn and now in theirs. The job was messy and smelly and he was sweating by the time he'd finished.

He was surprised when Justin and Sarah walked into the barn, hand in hand. She was smiling as if Justin had just caused the sun to set for her viewing pleasure. Justin wasn't wearing his hat, and his hair stuck up in the back with a cowlick that he'd had for as long as Noah could remember. His nose was sunburned, his pants a bit ragged at the hem and he'd spilled something from dinner on his shirt. Sarah didn't appear to notice any of those things.

It was obvious to anyone with eyes that they were crazy about one another, but since he'd been home Noah had come to understand that what these two shared went deeper than that. Neither was perfect, and he'd seen them argue a time or two. Regardless of the reason, within a few hours they'd be holding hands again. Maybe that was what Olivia Mae had meant. What was it she'd said when they were eating on her front porch? That all women want the same thing that men do—to be respected.

There was an obvious respect for each other between Justin and Sarah. Noah felt a twinge of envy. Who wouldn't?

"I thought you two were going to town."

"Already did. You've been out here awhile, bro."

Noah glanced around. The stalls were clean, fresh hay had been laid, all the buckets had water and the tools had been put back on their pegs. When had he done all of that? How long had he been in the barn? He glanced through the open door and saw the sky darkening, so it must be after eight. Yeah, he'd been in the barn a couple of hours.

Instead of explaining that he'd lost track of time, he said, "It's been a long day. Think I'll go in and clean up."

"Actually we wanted to talk to you." Sarah nodded her head toward the chairs set out under the tall sycamore tree. "Maybe over there, where there's a breeze?"

"I can't be in trouble. I haven't been home long enough today to do anything but eat and muck stalls."

"Don't be so defensive," Justin said.

"*Ya.* Maybe we just like hanging out with you." Sarah bumped her shoulder against his.

He'd only known his brother's wife a few weeks, but already he could tell that she was good for Justin and easy to get along with. The three of them sat under the tree, Justin and Sarah in the bench swing, and Noah in the metal lawn chair. He realized that he hadn't really taken the time to do this since he'd been home—to just sit and be with his family. It seemed that he'd spent the last ten years running away from things, or running toward them, but never being still.

A firefly sparked in front of him, then another.

Somewhere near the porch a bullfrog croaked. A songbird called out to its mate—short, urgent notes that were quickly answered. Noah tipped back his head and studied the stars that he could see through the branches of the tree.

After a few moments, he said, "This is nice, but I suspect there's something you want to say to me."

"Well, now that you mention it…" Sarah placed her hand on top of her stomach. "We know that the family has been pushing you to court."

"*Pushing* is a *gut* word for it."

"Yup. They're 'all up in your business.'" Justin laughed at the phrase that even Amish *youngies* used. "But you know it's because they care."

"Uh-huh." He was getting a bad feeling about this talk.

"Don't look so defensive," Sarah said.

"How does a person look defensive?"

"Like that…crossing your arms tight and frowning so hard I'm pretty sure there's a wrinkle between your eyes."

Which made him laugh. The last thing he was worried about was wrinkles.

Sarah cleared her throat and smiled. "We just want you to know that we approve of Olivia Mae."

"What?" He nearly came out of the lawn chair, then eased back and forced himself to not cross his arms tightly. "What are you talking about?"

"Only that we think you two would make a good match." Justin put his arms across the back of the swing. "We want to be encouraging."

"And offer to help, so if she, you know, needs help with her grandparents so that she can get away, we'd be happy to sit with them."

Had they been eavesdropping on his and Olivia Mae's conversation? But that was impossible. He'd been at her house. The Amish grapevine was good, but it wasn't that good. Only the sheep could have overheard them. Sarah was a good guesser, or maybe she'd read the situation better than he had. Maybe it wasn't a guess after all.

"Actually, we are going out tomorrow."

Sarah looked up at Justin. "See? I told you."

"Uh-uh. It's not like that. It's another lesson."

"A lesson?" Justin shook his head, as if he wasn't about to fall for that.

"Didn't you just have one of those?" Sarah reached her foot forward and pushed the swing into motion. "Must be going really well."

"And you two must be awfully bored if you want to spend your free time teasing me."

"We're not teasing." Justin glanced at his wife. "And it was her idea, to offer to sit with Abe and Rachel. After what you shared at dinner, it sounds like Olivia Mae could use some help."

He had mentioned the doctor's assessment at dinner. He'd forgotten about that.

"I'm sure she could use some help," Noah admitted. "And I don't know why she hasn't asked for it up until now—embarrassed, I guess."

"Or in denial." Sarah nodded her head so hard that her *kapp* strings bounced. "I know a little about that."

He suddenly remembered the situation Sarah had been in before Olivia Mae had matched her with Justin. She'd been the sole caretaker for an elderly *aenti*. When the *aenti* had passed, Sarah hadn't known what she was going to do. She didn't have any other family, and she'd tried maintaining the home by herself. It was only when Olivia Mae had stopped over for a visit that the community had understood how in need Sarah was.

Justin had shared all of this when Noah had first come home, but he hadn't really thought about it until now. Maybe Sarah did know something about what Olivia Mae was going through. Perhaps the two of them would make good friends.

"I appreciate your vote of approval, but Olivia Mae and I are just friends."

"So that's why you spent all day repairing her roof, because you're *gut* friends?"

"Was I supposed to leave it like it was, leaking?"

"We have groups who do home repairs for those who can't. You could have let Lucas know, and he would have seen that it was taken care of—"

Noah shook his head before Justin could finish. "It only took a couple of hours."

"But you were gone all day," Sarah said softly.

"Yeah, I know I was. I wanted to wait and see what the doctor had to say. I was worried about her." He lifted his hands, palms out. "I was worried about my *friend*."

Sarah and Justin shared a look between them that he couldn't read. Pushing herself to her feet, Sarah stood, stretched and walked to where he was sitting. She put a hand on his shoulder, and said, "Just don't wait too long to make up your mind."

Make up my mind?

Maybe Sarah had spent too much time in the sun today. She wasn't making a lot of sense.

Justin hopped up to follow her in, but held back a minute. "I don't know how she knows things like that."

"Like what?"

"You being in love with Olivia Mae."

"I'm not in love—"

"Women. It's like they have a sixth sense about these things." He slapped Noah on the back and followed his wife into the house, leaving Noah to stare up at the stars and wonder if they were right.

Was he in love with Olivia Mae Miller?

Chapter Ten

It was past nine o'clock when Olivia Mae finally went to her room, pulled off her *kapp* and unbraided her hair. Massaging her scalp, she tried to relax, but she was too keyed up. Too much had happened in one day. She would never be able to sleep if she went to bed now.

So she tried knitting. When she'd dropped a stitch three different times, she frogged the row she'd been working on, reinserted her needles in the previous row's loops and put the project back in her bag.

Perhaps she should try reading, but when she picked up the book from the library with the Christian romance sticker on the side, she simply held it and stared out the window. The man and woman on the cover caused a deep yearning to stir in her heart. She loved matching people together, but she was rather practical about it.

When the people she put together were meant to be a couple, it seemed that the emotions followed. But what did she really know about falling in love? How did it feel to trust someone else with your hurts and dreams and feelings?

She put the book back on her dresser and picked up the one *Mammi* had given her the previous Christmas. But even the book on sheep trivia didn't hold her attention. As Olivia Mae paged through it, she kept thinking of Noah and his silly jokes.

She thought of him on top of their roof, his hat pulled low over his eyes.

Could practically see him as he reached for the reins of Zeus and said, *I'll take care of the horse.*

She could see him smiling at her as she told him about the sheep.

Why was she thinking about Noah Graber? He was a friend, a fellow church member, someone she was trying to match. She had no reason to let her thoughts drift off any of those paths.

So instead she jumped up and began straightening items in her already tidy room. It was while she was dusting off the top of her dresser that she found the letter box Noah had brought to her house nearly a month ago.

Sinking onto her bed, she pushed back the

covers, sat cross-legged and held the box in her lap.

She ran her fingers over the soft wood, the engraved butterflies and finally the clasp.

Pulling in a deep breath, she opened it and upended the letters in her lap. She still remembered how clever she felt at the time that she'd written them. All of the other girls her age were keeping a diary, but she had decided to write letters to herself. In the back of her mind, she'd pictured herself years in the future—sitting in a new home with her husband and children scattered throughout the rooms. In the daydream, she'd occasionally receive a letter from herself, as if she could have mailed it from the past.

Powerless to resist the pull of her own handwriting, the words of her younger self, she picked up the first sheet, unfolded it and began to read.

June 8
Staying with Mammi and Daddi is my favorite part of summer. It's so much better than being at home, where my bruders roughhouse and fart and laugh at stupid jokes. It's no easy thing being the only girl in a house full of boys. When I get married, my husband is going to have good manners

and enjoy the things I enjoy—like reading and taking walks and watching sunsets.

June 17
Suzanne told Martha who told me that Suzanne's brother likes me. I'm not sure how I feel about that, but I'm keeping an open mind.

June 18
Suzanne and Martha and I were sitting in the back of the barn during the singing tonight. Richard came over and asked if he could sit beside me. He held my hand during the last song, but afterward he went back to his friends. They were laughing, and he looked over at me a few times.

Does he like me?

Does he want to be my beau?

I wish I had an older schweschder to talk to. Mammi's too old to remember courting.

June 25
Richard kissed me tonight.

I think I might be falling in love.

June 28
Today might have been the worst day of my life. I didn't mean to eavesdrop, but

that didn't stop me from hearing, and as Mammi is fond of saying, you can't unhear something so be careful what you listen to.

How I wish I had followed that advice.

Only I am glad that I heard. Otherwise I would have gone on believing that Richard actually liked me. Instead I know it was just a dare. I was coming back from using the outhouse. As I came around the corner, I saw them all standing together and heard someone mention my name. I jumped backward, curious and embarrassed at the same time. I was close enough to hear, though—to hear and recognize who was speaking.

Richard's friend laughed and said, "You should date her. Honest. I hear a plump wife and a big barn never did any man harm."

I thought I might die right there, but I knew boys could be rude. Don't I have five bruders? It didn't bother me, what Richard's friend said. But then I heard Richard speak over their laughter.

"Nope, the slender kind is more my type. Now pay up. I kissed her like you dared me to."

I should have known he couldn't really be interested in me.

No one our age wants a plump wife.

No one wants me.
I want to go home.

The letters weren't in any particular order. She relived that summer in random sequence, relived the hopes and dreams and disappointments. Finally, she read the last one, folded up the letters, slipped them back into the box and closed the lid.

But she didn't put the box up.

Instead she turned out her light and sat there in the dark, moonlight spilling in through her window, her mind traveling back to that summer when she'd written the letters to herself, when she'd first fallen in love, when she'd felt beautiful and womanly.

She'd thought the letters would be like writing to a best friend or a sister.

She'd thought it would be fun—that someday she'd look back and laugh at her younger self. That she'd be amazed at how young and bright and witty she was.

She could see now that she'd been a young girl with a fragile self-image. She had allowed a boy she barely knew to break her heart. She'd allowed her opinion of herself to be changed because of what a teenaged boy said to one of his buddies.

Was that why she'd never dated?

Why she'd always pushed away men?

Was that why she'd become a matchmaker?

She gently placed the box on top of the dresser and climbed back into bed, this time lying down and staring up at the ceiling.

She'd struggled with her weight as a teenager. As a young adult, she'd told herself it didn't matter. She remembered the year her mother had to sew new dresses for her because she couldn't let out the old ones she had any more. It wasn't a big deal. Many Amish girls carried an extra twenty pounds, though by that time all of Olivia Mae's friends were dating or married.

She flopped over onto her side and stared out the window.

When she'd moved in with her grandparents, she'd worked harder than she ever had before. She'd also changed her diet—not from any misguided notion of attracting a beau, but because she'd been worried about her grandparents' health. The pounds slipped away, but the image she had of herself had remained the same. She was no longer heavy, but neither was she *slender*—Richard's word caused her to cringe.

She could see now that in some ways she was still a young girl, on the brink of womanhood, pining away for Richard Hofstetter.

She jumped up, snagged her brush from the

top of her dresser and sat down in the single rocking chair in her room. Pulling her hair over her shoulder, she stared down at it. As a young girl, she'd loved to watch her mother brush her own hair each evening. It had reached well past her waist, and Olivia Mae thought it was the stuff of fairy tales. She'd thought of her mother as an Amish Rapunzel, only she didn't need to be saved because she had a happy home, a loving husband, a family.

Remembering her mother didn't bring the pain it once had. She still missed her parents, still wished she could speak with them, but she knew she would—one day. They'd be reunited in the next life. She didn't doubt that for a moment, and it eased the loneliness in her heart.

Her hair was now longer than her mother's was then, though most of the blond strands had darkened to brown. She brushed it, one hundred strokes, the same as her mother had always done, then she plaited it into a loose braid.

She'd changed.

She wasn't the young girl who had written those letters. She was a woman now. Maybe it was time—past time—to accept that she wasn't a chubby young girl that no man would want anymore.

Maybe it was time to stop being a matchmaker, to stop focusing on finding happiness for others and to start living her own life.

Just maybe it was time to allow herself to dream.

A home health-care nurse came by the house the next afternoon. Jeanette Allen was a large woman, wearing loose-fitting blue jeans and a top that was a soft purple and featured cats playing with balls of yarn. It was soon obvious to Olivia Mae that Jeanette was comfortable with herself and very good at her job.

She had a checklist and went through the house marking things on her clipboard. When she'd finished, she joined *Mammi* and Olivia Mae in the kitchen.

"You have a beautiful home."

"Danki." *Mammi* placed a platter of oatmeal cookies on the table.

Olivia Mae fixed a cup of coffee for each of them.

"So did we pass?" Olivia Mae asked.

Mammi was more specific with her question. "We don't have to move him, do we? Because Olivia Mae and I, we're determined to keep Abe here as long as possible, and—being Amish and all—we don't often resort to nursing homes."

"It's not a pass-or-fail thing. I understand that you'd rather keep him here, and that isn't my call, anyway. If I were to find your home to be a neglectful or unsafe environment, then I would be required to report that to my supervisor, who would report it to the authorities, but it's obvious that isn't the case."

She smiled at them both, waited for her words to sink in and then continued. "I can tell that you're doing your very best to care for Mr. Lapp."

She sipped the coffee and accepted a cookie when *Mammi* pushed the plate toward her. "There are things that you can do to make life easier for Mr. Lapp. Would he like to join us as we discuss those?"

"He's resting," *Mammi* said. "Days when he takes a nap, well, they're better for all of us. He seems less…aggravated."

"Understandable. All right. Let's see what I've checked here."

Most of the items were obvious, and Olivia Mae was a little embarrassed that she hadn't thought of them earlier.

Remove the rugs so that *Daddi* doesn't trip.

Place red tape on the floor around the stove they used to heat the living room in winter and also on the handles of the stove and oven in the kitchen.

Keep all medications out of reach and make sure they have child-resistant lids.

Avoid stacks of old newspapers or other clutter that cause anxiety and represent a tripping hazard.

Install a handrail on both sides of the front-porch steps and in the bathroom.

"It's a lot," *Mammi* said.

"But most of these things are small." Olivia Mae felt empowered by the list. Finally, she understood that there were things they could do to make life easier and safer for all of them, to make living here possible—if only her brothers would agree to it.

Jeanette stayed another thirty minutes, going over dietary suggestions and support for caregivers. When Olivia Mae walked her out to her car, she said, "You're doing a good job here, Olivia Mae."

"I don't know about that."

"Trust me. I've seen all sorts of home situations. What you've done here, without any guidance, is very good."

"I have five *bruders* in Maine. They all think we should move closer to them."

"It might be a good idea. I don't recommend that you—or any caregiver—try to handle such a situation on their own, and your grandmother is going to need additional care as the years pass. They both will."

"One day at a time," Olivia Mae murmured.

"Yes, that's a good thing to keep in mind, but we also have to keep an eye on the future. You know, too often I see situations like this wear down a caregiver—women who are forty and look sixty, women who were in good health suddenly dealing with back problems and anxiety and sleeplessness." She opened the door to her car, but she didn't get in. "If your brothers are willing to help, let them. Anyone who is willing to help, they're a gift from God."

Winking, she got into her car. "I'm not supposed to make religious comments, but I didn't think I'd offend you."

"*Nein.* You didn't."

"Good. I'll see you next week."

Olivia Mae watched the sleek gray car drive away. One more person who thought they should move. It seemed everyone thought it was a good idea but her. So maybe she was being stubborn. Maybe she was too close to the problem to see things clearly.

Noah directed Snickers down Olivia Mae's lane at exactly six o'clock. He was having second thoughts about inviting her out to dinner. Olivia Mae was dealing with a lot right now. Why did he think she'd like to go out for a night on the town? No doubt she'd accepted out of pity for him.

Unless...

But his mind froze as soon as the word *unless* entered. He simply couldn't see beyond his doubts and bad experiences.

She was waiting on the porch, wearing her customary light gray dress and white apron. She was smiling, though. Surely that was something. As soon as he stopped the gelding, she walked down the steps, but he hopped out of the buggy before she reached him.

"Would it be okay if I go inside a minute? Just to say hello to Abe."

The old guy had been on his mind nearly as much as Olivia Mae had. Noah had never seen anyone enjoy a game of checkers so much.

Olivia Mae seemed surprised at his request, but she nodded and walked back up onto the porch. When they stepped into the living room, something looked different, something he couldn't put his finger on. Of course, the pots and bowls were gone, but there was something else that had changed.

Then he snapped his fingers. "You took out the rugs."

"Apparently they're a tripping hazard," Rachel said. She glanced at Abe, smiled and then turned her attention back to Noah. "I have some coffee on the stove. I could heat it up if you'd like a cup."

"*Nein*. We're about to go and eat. I just wanted to say hello."

Abe looked up from peas that he was shelling. "Hello. I'm Abe Lapp."

Noah stepped forward, taking off his hat as he did so. "Noah Graber."

"Do I know you?"

"*Ya*, I believe you do."

"Sometimes I can't remember."

"I'm the one who wants to forget—you thrashed me at checkers the other night."

Abe cocked his head as if he could capture the memory. Finally, he shrugged and said, "I was always *gut* at checkers."

Abe returned his attention to the peas, and Rachel picked up her knitting. "You two go on now. Have a nice evening."

"You're sure—"

"Olivia Mae, we'll be fine. Now shoo."

Olivia Mae turned to look at Noah, one eyebrow arched slightly higher than the other. "Did she just shoo me?"

"I think she did."

"I guess we should go then."

"We might as well."

Noah liked teasing Olivia Mae. He liked when she smiled and the worries she wore like a shawl fell away. He liked making her happy, and at the moment she definitely looked as if she was looking forward to the evening.

He started toward the door and then turned back toward Rachel. "My *bruder* and his wife are going to stop by in an hour or so, just to make sure everything is okay."

"It'll be nice to see them," Rachel said.

On the drive into town, he asked Olivia Mae about the nurse's visit. She told him the things they were going to change around the house and asked if he knew anyone who could install handrails for the porch and bathroom.

"I'll take care of it tomorrow."

"That's not what I meant."

"But I want to." The matter seemed to be settled. He was suddenly glad he hadn't accepted the offer to work one of the Saturday auctions. While the money probably would have been good, at this point he didn't need the money. But Olivia Mae did need the help.

When they reached the downtown area of Goshen, he said, "Where would you like to eat?"

"You haven't already picked the place?"

"*Nein.* My dating instructor says it's best to let the lady choose."

"Smart instructor."

"So I've heard."

Olivia Mae pretended to have a hard time deciding, but finally she leaned toward him and said, "I'd love pizza."

"Would you, now?"

"Not typical Amish food, I know, which is why I'd like it."

"You're not picking pizza because it's cheap?"

"We'll share a dessert if you just want to spend more money."

"Deal." He directed Snickers down Main Street and pulled into the parking area across the street from the town's most popular pizza spot. The place was packed, which wasn't surprising considering it was a Friday night. For some reason, that didn't irritate him like it had the last time he'd tried to eat there.

Instead he snagged two chairs at an outside table as soon as a couple left, and he waved wildly at Olivia Mae, who was standing in line. She shrugged, indicating she wasn't about to get out of line, and he couldn't leave the table.

It was a predicament! Then he remembered he was wearing a light jacket. He took it off, draped it over one of the chairs and accepted two glasses of water from the worker who was walking by. Orders were placed at the window, but several teens bussed tables and distributed glasses of water, silverware and napkins. Satisfied that no one would mistake their table for an empty one and grab it, he hurried over to Olivia Mae.

"How about you hold the table, and I'll place the order."

"I could place the order."

"But I want to pay."

"You don't have to pay. This isn't that kind of date."

"*Ya*, I know, but I want to."

An *Englisch* couple in front of them couldn't help overhearing their conversation.

"Sounds like our first date," the woman said.

The man nodded in agreement. "And our second."

"We finally agreed to take turns."

"*Gut* idea," Noah said. "I'll take the first turn."

"Fine. I'd like Canadian bacon and pineapple."

"Sounds disgusting."

"It's *gut*, I promise."

"We'll do half and half."

"What are you putting on your half?"

"Anchovies, of course."

She wrinkled her nose, then leaned forward and lowered her voice. "Never order anchovies while you're on a date."

He matched her tone, as if they were sharing an intimate secret. "I was kidding."

"You're sure?"

"*Ya.*"

"*Gut.* Your dating score is improving by the minute."

"Not so fast. You're not getting out of my third lesson." Whistling, he moved forward in the line, as she hurried back toward the table. Instead of paying attention to the menu posted overhead on a chalkboard, or the people in front of him, he kept peeking over at Olivia Mae. When she caught him watching her, he smiled, offered a little wave and turned to study the crowd.

About half of the teenagers—both Amish and *Englisch*—were tapping on their cell phones. People thought Amish teens didn't have cell phones, but of course many of them did. The difference was that their parents didn't pay for them. If a *youngie* wanted to work an extra five or ten hours a week to afford a phone, that was up to them. Noah didn't know a single family that allowed them in the house, though, so most teens kept them out on the porch or even in the barn. Noah had better things to spend his money on, like a bachelor pad or dinners with Olivia Mae.

Quite a few tables were occupied by families with young children. He glanced over at Olivia Mae again. She'd begun talking to a mother who was holding a young baby. If he wasn't imagining things, a look of yearning passed over Olivia Mae's face.

Why had she never married?

She would make a good wife, a good mother. Any man would be happy to have her by his side.

He shook away those thoughts as he stepped forward to place their order. He was helping a friend who needed a night away. It was nothing more than that, even if he wanted it to be.

The wait for their pizza passed too quickly. They never ran out of things to talk about, but they would occasionally lapse into silence, which was just as comfortable.

Dating was easy when he was with Olivia Mae. He felt none of the awkwardness that he'd suffered through with Jane and Francine.

It seemed they'd barely arrived, but already their dinner was finished, and he found himself looking for ways to avoid taking her home.

"Let's go for ice cream."

"I'm too full. I shouldn't have eaten that last slice of supreme."

"I told you that you'd like it."

"You did, and you were right, especially since it didn't include anchovies." She patted her stomach as if it was huge, which it wasn't.

"Ice cream would be *gut*. We can even share a scoop." When she looked at him like he was wearing his hat backward, he backpedaled. "Or get a small. We'll get a children's cone. Come on. I haven't had ice cream in ages."

She finally relented, declaring he was more persistent than a child. It was while they were sitting in front of the ice-cream shop—Olivia Mae holding a cone with strawberry ice cream and chocolate sprinkles, Noah enjoying a double dip of butter pecan—that she became serious about the subject of his dating.

"You know, Noah, I think I understand your problem."

He'd been chasing a dribble of ice cream down his cone, but now he froze and raised his eyes to hers.

"Don't look at me that way. I just meant I think I understand your issues with women." She rushed on when he tried to interrupt. "It's not that you need lessons. It's that you're an introvert."

"A what?"

"An introvert." She bit into the crunchy cone. "You know. Someone who is more comfortable alone."

"I don't know if that's true."

"Does being around a large group of people wear you out?"

"Like an Amish gathering, you mean? *Ya.* Sometimes."

"Do you prefer a few close friendships to a lot of casual ones?"

He thought about that a minute and finally admitted, "The only real friends I've ever had are my *bruders*."

"You're a *gut* listener, and you seem to think before you talk—usually."

"*Danki*. I guess."

"It's not bad to be an introvert."

"What are you?"

"Maybe a mixture of the two, but if I had to choose? Introvert. I tend to look at life from the inside out."

"I don't know what that means."

"You know." She tapped her chest. "I think about what people are feeling before I think about what they're doing or saying. Of course, we can't always know what someone else is feeling, so life can be hard for an introvert."

"Are you saying it's hopeless?"

"I'm saying that when you're comfortable with someone, like I think you're comfortable with me, then you act normal. You don't feel as if you have to cover every silence with words, and you haven't told a single animal joke tonight."

"I thought you liked my jokes."

"Uh-huh."

"I see what you mean, I guess." In truth he knew that his *problem* wasn't that simple. If Olivia Mae knew the truth about him, if she knew his past, she wouldn't think the *problem* was as simple as what personality type he was.

Chapter Eleven

Olivia Mae had been enjoying herself for the first time in a long time when Noah's mood suddenly changed. He tossed his unfinished cone into the trash, said it was getting late and walked her back to the buggy without another word.

She didn't understand what had happened.

She'd thought he was enjoying the night as much as she was.

As they drove back to her house, an uncomfortable silence filled the buggy. Noah drove as if the road required every ounce of his attention.

He didn't smile.

Didn't speak.

Didn't tell a single joke.

Could it be that she'd misread the entire situation? It had started to feel like a real date, but perhaps he didn't think of her that way. Perhaps he was just slogging through his commitment to the deal he'd made with his mother. Maybe, just maybe, he wasn't interested in a plump wife.

Nein.

Whatever had changed his mood, she was pretty sure it had nothing to do with her and Noah, and it certainly had nothing to do with her weight. That insecurity was her past, exerting itself into her present. She didn't have to allow that. She didn't have to let her old fears and old hurts ruin a perfectly good evening.

When they reached her grandparents' farm, Noah helped her out of the buggy, murmured "good night" and then strode back around to the driver's side.

She thought about letting him go.

But something told her that tonight was a chance she didn't want to let slip away. A chance for what, she didn't know, but she followed her instinct. "If you have a minute, I'd like you to stay."

"Stay?"

"Sit on the porch with me. I need to run inside and check on *Mammi* and *Daddi*, but I'd like... I'd like to talk to you a minute."

If anything, Noah looked more miserable than he had on the buggy ride home, but he nodded in agreement so she hurried into the house.

Daddi was already in bed sleeping.

Mammi was sitting in her rocker, an open Bible in her lap and a cup of tea on the table beside her.

Telling her grandmother to holler if she needed anything, Olivia Mae grabbed a dark green shawl from the hook by the door and walked back outside. She almost took a lantern, but she had a feeling that Noah would be more comfortable speaking if he didn't have to look directly at her.

She stopped to close the screen door quietly, stood there in the pool of light and Noah said, "That color looks *gut* on you."

Her heart tripped a beat. *"Danki."*

"Did you make it?"

"Ya."

"From your sheep wool?"

"Nein. I never did buy a spinner. The whole thing was too expensive. So I sell the wool, and use the money to buy more yarn." She didn't add that this was a sweater she'd purchased from the thrift store, frogged and reworked into a light shawl. Admitting that a week ago might have stirred the old ache in her heart for what could have been, but now it seemed trivial. It was unimportant. She understood that Noah meant the compliment, but he was stalling.

She sat down in the rocker beside him and said, "Explain to me what happened."

"When?"

"Earlier. At the ice-cream shop, when you went quiet."

She thought he might refuse her. He set the chair to rocking, stared out at the night and finally ran a hand up and across the back of his neck, massaging the muscles there.

"What you said about my being an introvert, that might be true. It might be part of it, but it's not all of it."

"What do you mean?"

"If you knew my history, you'd understand that it's nothing as simple as personality type."

"So explain it to me—explain what you mean by your *history*."

Instead of answering, Noah dropped his head into his hands.

Olivia Mae waited a minute, then two. Finally she said, "It's not that bad, Noah."

"How do you know?"

"Because the moon is still shining."

His head jerked up, he looked out over the porch railing, out into the cool summer evening, and then back at Olivia Mae. "You're saying the world goes on."

"I'm saying that sometimes things seem worse when they're stuck in our head, going round and round." She thought of the letters still in the box in her room. She'd let those doubts and fears and hurts trouble her for too long. Why was she free of them now? What had changed?

She couldn't say.

She only knew it felt good not to carry that weight any longer.

"Tell me," she said. "Not because I need to know, but because I think you'll feel better when you do."

He stood up, walked to the railing, turned to look at her, then strode back across the porch and plopped into the rocker. When he began to speak, she understood that it took all of the courage he had to do so. She understood that the trust he was showing in her was a precious thing.

"When I first left Goshen, I was young—only nineteen. I had some vision of myself traveling from community to community, enjoying the free life. In Maine, I worked on a farm helping with the harvest. The farmer had a daughter..."

He must have sensed her smile, because he said, "I know. Sounds like a bad country song. Cora was younger than I was at the time—only seventeen. I didn't want a serious relationship. I wasn't looking for that at all, and I thought I'd made my intentions clear. I was still seeing myself out on the road with no obligations, able to pack up and move whenever the mood struck me, which I did a few weeks later when the harvest was done."

"You broke her heart?"

Olivia Mae could only see the outline of Noah, the shape of him. But a lot could be observed from a person's posture, the way they held their head, the tightness of their shoulders. At her words, Noah looked up, sharply, but then it seemed to her that the tension in his features eased. She could have imagined that, but she didn't imagine his voice, which was softer now, softer and tired.

"*Ya.* I suppose I did. The bad part is that I think I knew I was doing it as I was doing it, but it was just such a heady thing to have a girl like me, to have her want to spend the rest of her life with me. Here in Goshen, I'd always been Caleb's younger brother."

"I haven't met Caleb," she said softly, just to keep him talking.

"He's the oldest. Lives in Nappanee now—close enough to visit. All my *bruders* live close enough to visit. Maybe that's why I wanted to get away. Here, I was always going to be just another one of those Graber boys. There? Well, there I was something special." He sat back, again set the chair to rocking. "But it wasn't enough to convince me to stay in Maine. I didn't

even tell Cora a proper goodbye. I told myself
that it would be better that way. I just left."

"Introverts avoid confrontation."

"I guess. Maybe I was just a coward."

"You're being a little hard on yourself."

"Then there was Samantha." He sat forward,
elbows on his knees, fingers interlaced. "She
was *Englisch*, and I pretended I was, too, which
was a joke. Anyone could tell from the way I
talk that I'm Amish, but Samantha... Well, she
just accepted whatever I said. I even bought
some blue jeans and T-shirts, let my hair grow
out, wore a fancy pair of sunglasses that must
have looked ridiculous. It was almost as if I
needed to be someone else, something else."

"Why do you think that was?"

"It was like I was running from who I was.
What did I know? I was probably twenty-one
or twenty-two, and at that time I really had no
idea what I wanted my future to look like or
who I wanted to be. So who knows what I was
running from? Shadows maybe."

"You're not the first *youngie* to have an iden-
tity crisis."

"Sure. I guess that's true, and it's kind of you
to say so. But that doesn't explain Ida. I was old
enough to know better with her. It was only two
years ago."

"You don't have to talk about this if you don't want to."

"Maybe you were right, though, when you said I'll feel better if I do. Maybe confession is good for the soul." He stood again, paced up and down the porch and finally stopped in front of her, leaning back against the porch railing, arms crossed, eyes studying her. It was as if he needed to see her response more than he needed to hide because of his embarrassment.

"Ida was an Amish girl I met when I was working at an auction house in New York. It was a *gut* community, and I learned quickly that the auction work was something I was able to do well, something I enjoyed."

"And Ida?"

"Daughter of the main auctioneer." He crossed his legs at the ankles, recrossed his arms as if he could get more comfortable, stared up at the ceiling and finally shook his head. "It would have been a nice place to settle, and Ida—she was a sweet girl. I don't actually remember asking her to marry, but suddenly we were pledged and attending classes with the bishop."

"You didn't ask her? But you were pledged?"

Noah only shrugged, as if even he didn't understand what had happened. "Before I knew it, the big day arrived. I thought I could do it. I thought everything would be all right afterward, that my feelings for her would be what they were supposed to be."

"What did you do?"

"What I always do—I ran. The morning of our wedding, I crept out of the house before dawn and hit the road—hitchhiked to Kentucky. That's what I'm telling you, what I've been trying to tell you. There's something wrong with me, and it's not just that I'm an introvert."

Olivia Mae had been sitting, patiently listening. But she couldn't sit any longer when she heard the desperation in Noah's voice. She smoothed out her dress, stood, walked across the porch and stopped next to him, mirroring his posture, which meant they were both staring back into the house. She watched as *Mammi* set aside her Bible and walked into her bedroom, leaving the lantern on for her.

"So let me get this straight." She ticked off the items on her fingers. "You're a heartbreaker, you avoid confrontation at all costs and you run whenever you feel backed into a corner."

"*Ya*, I guess that sums it up."

She stared at her three fingers. "I think we're each allowed a few flaws—at least three."

"You're making light of this and you know it."

"Actually I'm trying not to lecture you."

"Is that so?"

"Yes." She turned toward him, studied his

profile. "Noah, there is nothing wrong with you. Cora and Samantha? You were too young to know what you wanted or how you felt. I know. Don't even say it. I know that many of our friends marry that young."

"Or younger."

"But many don't. And many, like you and me... Well, it takes longer. Some people are older when they fall in love and maybe that's because it takes a while for them—for us—to know their hearts."

"But what of Ida? I was older by that time, certainly older than her. I should have known better."

"Sometimes we end up in situations that we don't know how to get out of. The way you left, that was wrong and you should write her an apology. Whether she accepts it or not, that's her choice. But not marrying her? If you didn't love her, then you shouldn't have married her."

"Not everyone marries for love."

"That's true. Sometimes those relationships work out and sometimes they don't, but you knew you didn't love her. That's a form of dishonesty and basing a marriage on that? Never a *gut* idea."

He finally turned toward her, searched her face in the little bit of light that spilled out through the window.

"Why are you doing this?"

"Doing what?" She tried not to react to the way he was looking at her, to the way his eyes searched hers.

"Trying to make me feel better."

"Isn't that what a friend is supposed to do?"

"Is that what we are—friends?"

When she didn't answer, he stepped closer. Olivia Mae's heart rate accelerated like one of her sheep tearing across the pasture.

"Olivia, may I…"

This time she didn't admonish him for playing with her name. Instead she nodded. He reached out and touched her face, and she thought she might melt right into the floor of the porch. And then he did what she'd been hoping for some time he would do. He kissed her softly, gently, and then more urgently. When she thought that her knees would give way completely, he pressed his forehead to hers.

Then without another word, he turned and walked out into the night.

Noah thought about that kiss for days.

He thought about it on Saturday as he installed railings next to her grandparents' porch steps and then in the bathroom adjacent to their bedroom. He thought about it on Sunday when he sat next to Olivia Mae at the church gathering. Then later, as they walked around Widow King's property, he thought about it and found the courage to hold her hand.

The widow's home was actually across from Noah's parents'. He had known her all his life. Known her when all of the children were still there. By the time her husband died, the eldest son had already taken over the working of the farm. He'd married and they now had a full household of children.

"Why doesn't she live in the *grossdaddi haus*?" Olivia Mae asked.

"She did, when her husband was alive. I guess she got lonely. A few years ago she moved back into the main house."

"So the *daddi* house is empty?"

"Looks like it."

They'd reached the small front porch, which was just big enough to hold two rockers. The door was unlocked—Amish rarely locked their doors and never their outbuildings. Olivia Mae threw a smile back at him and then walked into the house.

"Cute," she said.

"Small."

"Only two people in a *grossdaddi haus*. It's big enough."

The place was well laid out, built with large windows and high ceilings. The open windows caught the summer breeze and stepping inside was like stepping back into spring.

There was a fine layer of dust on the furniture, but overall the place was surprisingly clean. Of course, with only four rooms that couldn't have been too hard.

They walked through the sitting room, the bedroom, peeked into the bath and ended up in the kitchen.

"It's a *gut* house—nice and solid." Olivia Mae smiled up at him.

"No leaks in the roof."

"Ha. And no steps out front. It's designed for grandparents. They did a *gut* job."

He wanted to stay there with her—sit on the couch and pretend the place was theirs. The thought surprised him. Had he fallen in love with Olivia Mae? Could he see himself spending the rest of his life with her?

The next two days passed with excruciating slowness, though he was plenty busy. Their date—their final lesson—was scheduled for Wednesday night. He wanted to do something special, but he kept coming up blank.

They'd had dinner at her place.

He'd taken her out to pizza.

And she'd warned him against picnics.

So what was left? He was stewing over it as he worked in the family garden on Tuesday evening.

Justin came up behind him and let out a long low whistle. "What did that trowel ever do to you?"

"What do you mean?" Noah stared at the tool in his hand, then the row, then his brother.

"You're using it like a hammer. Thought maybe it had offended you in some way."

"Guess my mind was elsewhere."

"Did you and Olivia Mae have a fight?"

"What? *Nein.* It's just that... Well, we're supposed to have our final lesson tomorrow, and I can't decide where I should take her or what I should do. I want it to be special." He didn't add that he wanted it to be a real date and not just a lesson.

"Take her to your work," Justin said.

"Why would I do that?"

"She probably doesn't get out of Goshen much. I bet she'd enjoy a trip over to Shipshe. She could walk through the market and shop, maybe after she watches you auction."

"I don't think she'll leave Rachel and Abe for that long."

"I can take Sarah over to stay with them a few hours."

"She would do that?"

"Of course. She's been a little restless the last few days. It would probably cheer her up."

He had to admit the idea had merit. When he said that he'd run it by Olivia Mae, Justin grinned as if he'd stumbled upon the golden goose.

"What?"

"Nothing. Just nice to see you falling for someone."

Was he?

Falling for Olivia Mae?

He didn't know. He only knew that when he wasn't with her, he thought about the next time he would be with her. And when he was with her, he didn't want the time to end. But their date was the following evening. He couldn't count on her checking the phone shack, so he harnessed Snickers and drove over to her place.

He didn't want to show up empty-handed, so he stopped at the local farmer's market and purchased a basket of strawberries. She'd said something about needing to serve her grandparents more fruit.

She was standing in the kitchen, thanking him and washing the strawberries in the sink, when he brought up the subject of their next date.

"I was thinking you could come to the market."

"Market?"

"The flea market and auction house—in Shipshe."

"Why would I do that?"

"To see where I work. To get out for a little while."

"Oh, I don't know. That would be a long time for *Mammi* and *Daddi* to be alone."

"We're not children," *Mammi* said from the kitchen table, where she was cutting up slices of peach pie for each of them.

"I know you're not, but what if something happened?"

"Like what?" Noah winked at Rachel and she grinned back at him.

"*Ya*, like what? We're old people. We can't exactly get in trouble anymore. Takes more energy than I have, and Abe, I'm not sure he remembers how."

It was good to hear her joke about their situation. At least, Noah thought it was a good sign.

"See? She wants you to go, and Sarah offered to come by. Something about asking your *mammi* to show her how to bind off a blanket. I have no idea what that means."

Olivia Mae rolled her eyes, obviously not buying the idea that Sarah needed help with her knitting. But she also hesitated, as if she was considering going.

"I have to leave early in the day," Noah added. "But another bus heads that way just after the noon hour. You could catch that one, watch my auction at two o'clock, and then we could walk around through the flea market and have an early dinner. The last bus leaves Shipshe at six. You'd be home by seven."

"Never know what you might find," *Mammi* chimed in. "I like the idea. You might even come across more sweaters to buy on the cheap and frog."

Frogging made no more sense than *bind off* to Noah, but he nodded in agreement.

"Okay. Fine." Olivia Mae raised her hands in surrender. "Now let's eat some of that pie before the ice cream melts all over the table."

He hadn't meant to stay for two hours, but he did.

They talked about a number of things: her *daddi*'s health—it seemed to have stabilized. Her *mammi*'s episodes—she'd only had two since changing her medications. The sale of the farm—no one had expressed an interest yet.

Noah didn't want to think about Olivia Mae moving. So he told her about the newborn calves at his brother's place, how well the hay was coming in at his *dat*'s, and that he'd written letters of apology to Cora, Samantha and Ida.

"That's *gut*, Noah. That's really *gut*."

He kissed her again before he left.

And as he drove away he felt, finally, as if his life was on the correct track again—the track he'd deviated from over ten years ago.

Olivia Mae was ridiculously excited about her afternoon in Shipshe.

She dug out one of her cloth shopping bags and put it next to her purse. She counted the money she'd been saving from her sheep's wool and decided she could afford to spend twenty dollars. She made an early supper for her grandparents, set it in the icebox and left Sarah instructions for how to warm it up. As if Sarah didn't know how to warm up a chicken casserole.

At a few minutes before the noon hour, Justin showed up to drop off Sarah and also to take Olivia Mae to the bus station.

"It's nice of you to do this," she said to them both.

"Happy to." Sarah grinned and held up her knitting bag. "I really do need help with this project."

Mammi had taught Olivia Mae everything she knew about yarn, patterns and stitches. More important, she'd taught her to love knitting and, although her arthritis sometimes kept her from doing as much as she would like to do, she still enjoyed every aspect of it. Her eyes were sparkling as she told Sarah, "Come in. Come in and let's sit around the table."

Daddi was taking a nap, so Olivia Mae didn't wake him. She pushed the list of emergency instructions into Sarah's hands, whispered *"Danki"* and hurried out to the buggy.

Thirty minutes later she was on the way to Shipshewana.

When was the last time she'd taken an entire afternoon off for herself? She always tried to limit her errands to an hour, two at the most. The thought of an entire afternoon and evening to do with as she pleased made her positively giddy. And the thought of spending it with Noah? Well, that was icing on the cake.

The market had grown since she'd last been there. Of course, it had been years, but still she was surprised. She hopped off the bus and hurried toward the auction barn. Noah had told her that he'd be working the livestock auction. When she stepped into the cool shade of the auction area, she was nearly overwhelmed by the earthy smell of animals and hay and even manure. She saw crates of chickens, goats, several donkeys and, of course, sheep.

Then she heard his voice, and hurried toward the northeast corner of the barn. Noah was just beginning the afternoon auction. Olivia Mae's heart felt as if it had lodged itself in her throat when she saw him. He was dressed the same as always—straw hat, white long-sleeved shirt rolled up at the sleeves, dark pants and suspenders.

He noticed her, tipped his hat and then turned his attention to the people gathered around. He greeted everyone, said they'd be starting with a nice set of rabbits and then he began the opening bid.

And in that moment, when she first heard his auctioneer voice, Olivia Mae fell so hard and so completely that she knew resistance was a fool's game. The rhythm of his auctioneer's chant, the obvious fun he was having and the fact that she could stand back and watch everyone watch him shed an entirely new light on Noah Graber.

"Who'll give me ten? Ten-dollar bid?" he began. "Now twenty, now twenty, who will give me more?

"Twenty-dollar bid, now thirty, now thirty, will you give me forty? Thirty dollars for two breeders—how about thirty-two? Thirty-five? I got it! How about forty? Forty? Forty? I've got thirty-five. And these bunnies are hopping straight toward the fella in the Cubs baseball cap."

Laughter rippled through the growing crowd. Before it could die down, Noah was opening the bid on half a dozen goats. That was followed by crates of chickens, including a rooster that they let out to strut around as Noah called out to the crowd, "Don't be shy, don't let these big birds pass you by."

The auction passed so quickly that Olivia Mae looked around in surprise as people began to move away. Had she really been standing there for an hour? Noah had a break before his next auction so he walked around the flea market with her, bought her a snow cone and insisted on carrying her bag of yarn. The variegated blue cotton was on clearance and she'd spent her entire twenty dollars in one booth, but the joy of it washed over her.

How long had it been since she'd splurged on new yarn?

How long had it been since she'd purchased something merely because the color caught her eye and the feel of it sent her imagination running off in new directions?

Amish and *Englisch* walked alongside each other, peering into booths, enjoying homemade samples of salsa and bread and peanut butter.

"We're going to be too full for dinner," she said as she scooped the last dollop of peanut butter out of the tiny cup with the tiny spoon. It reminded her of the miniature ice-cream cups they used to buy from the truck that drove around their neighborhood.

"Maybe you'll have to help me in the next auction." Noah bumped his shoulder against hers. "Then you'll be hungry. Auctions always give me an appetite."

"That's because you're working hard."

"Do you think so?"

"*Ya*. You make it look like you're not working. You make it seem like you're up there having fun, but it's hard work to keep an auction going and keep everyone involved. Your auctions—they draw the biggest crowds."

Noah looped his arm through hers. "I like it here. I like this kind of work. But you know what I like even more?"

"What?"

"The fact that you came with me today."

Which seemed to sum it all up.

When they were together, Olivia Mae felt as if the world had suddenly been filled with possibilities. Her problems faded into the background, and she forgot to worry. Instead she started thinking about her future.

Chapter Twelve

Noah finished his second auction for the day and tried not to stare at Olivia Mae, who was standing in the back smiling like she was at the state fair.

When the auction was over, they left the flea market and walked through some of the shops in downtown Shipshe. He realized that he liked being with her. He liked the way that she smiled at *Englischers* and waved at their children. He liked how she stopped to hold a door open for an elderly Amish woman. He liked everything about her.

"Let's eat at the Blue Gate," he said to her.

"You're kidding."

"I'm not."

"They serve huge plates of food."

"I worked up an appetite today. Didn't you?"

She started to laugh, and he realized he liked

that about her, too. "*Ya*. You got me there. I did, too."

So they made their way into the Blue Gate restaurant, a place that Noah had only been to a half-dozen times in his life. It was somewhere his family went to on special occasions—to celebrate someone's birthday or someone graduating from their little one-room schoolhouse. Once they'd even come to celebrate his parents' twentieth anniversary.

But this day was just as special as those.

They hadn't once referred to their time together as a *lesson*.

And something told Noah that this day, a plain old Wednesday in the first week of June, would be one he'd always remember.

He ordered the Amish country sampler, and they had a good laugh over that. Olivia Mae ordered a grilled meat-loaf sandwich with fries and a side salad.

When they were done, he insisted they split a piece of pie.

"I'm going to burst. Honest, I can't eat another thing."

But he'd caught her looking at a piece of chocolate peanut-butter pie that the waitress was carrying to a nearby table. So he ordered one. "And two more forks, please." The waitress had taken away their silverware when she cleared off their dinner plates.

It seemed curiously intimate, sharing a piece of pie.

Noah found himself wishing that the night could go on forever, but, of course, it couldn't. They had to hurry to catch the bus, then sat together laughing about different parts of their day.

When the bus pulled into Goshen, Justin was waiting for them, as he'd said he would be.

But something was wrong.

Noah knew it the minute he saw his brother's face.

Justin met them halfway between the buggy and the bus. "Abe's at the hospital—here in town."

"What happened?" Olivia Mae's voice shook and her eyes widened and she reached for Noah's hand. "Is he okay? Where's *Mammi*? When did this happen? How did it happen?"

"He fell. Tried to get out of bed by himself, and he fell."

"Is he okay?" Noah asked.

"I think so. They had to put in a dozen stitches—"

But Olivia Mae wasn't listening now. She was hurrying toward the buggy. Noah and Justin caught up, and Justin said, "I'll take you there.

Sarah's with him, and my *mamm* came, too. Lucas was on his way."

Olivia Mae sat there, back ramrod straight, eyes blinking rapidly, staring out the window but not seeing a thing. Watching her nearly broke Noah's heart. She might seem just fine to anyone else, might look as if she had pulled herself together quickly, donning the role of responsibility once again. But Noah understood how afraid she was and how much she was hurting. Her grandparents were everything to her.

They were the parents that she'd lost, the brothers who lived so far away. And in some ways *Mammi* was the sister she'd never had. In other words, they were her family—her immediate family. The people she shared coffee with each morning, a prayer at every meal and the daily ups and downs of life. Olivia Mae understood that her grandparents wouldn't live forever, but she loved them and she would miss them terribly when they were gone.

Not that Abe was in the grave just yet. If there was one thing Noah was sure of, it was that the old guy was tough and would fight through anything to stay with his family.

They rode in silence.

Justin drove.

Noah sat in the back with Olivia Mae.

He didn't ask if she was okay. He could tell

that she was afraid and worried and upset—but she was also calm after the initial shock.

He didn't tell her everything would be fine.

How was he to know that it would be?

But he held her hand, and when they reached the hospital, he jumped out of the buggy and hurried with her into the emergency room. Olivia Mae rushed straight to the information desk as if she'd been there before.

"I'm here to see my *daddi*—Abe." Her voice shook and her hands had begun to shake. She glanced at Noah, then back at the person manning the information desk, and tried again. "His name is Abe Lapp. He was brought in earlier tonight. Can you tell me where he is? Can you tell me if he's okay?"

Sarah must have heard Olivia Mae's voice. She must have been waiting for them because she came hurrying toward them before the receptionist could answer Olivia Mae's questions.

"We're down the hall," Sarah said. "All of us are…waiting just down the hall."

When they turned the corner into the main waiting room, Noah understood what she meant. He'd expected his *mamm* and Sarah and maybe Lucas—like his brother had said. But it seemed that word had traveled quickly. Ezra Yoder and Daniel King, their two preachers, were sitting near the window playing checkers. Half a dozen older folks occupied chairs along one wall—all Amish, all there to wait and pray. They must be friends of Rachel and Abe. This show of support was a testament to what a difference Olivia Mae's grandparents had made in the community. They were obviously well liked.

The expressions were somber, and he noticed several folks had their heads bowed in prayer.

Jane and Francine were also there. They rushed toward Olivia Mae and put their arms around her. Noah thought that perhaps she'd like to be alone with her friends, but when he turned to step away, she reached for his hand and led him toward Lucas.

"Is *Daddi* going to be okay?"

"*Ya*, he is." Lucas motioned to the seat beside him. Olivia Mae sat, but Noah remained standing.

"What happened? Justin said he fell. Said he needed quite a few stitches."

"Abe was trying to get out of bed, and apparently he wasn't quite awake yet. He lost his balance and went down hard. The cut on his head is a long one, and they had to shave his hair to stitch him up." He patted Olivia Mae's hand. "Sarah and Justin, they acted quickly. Sarah stayed with your grandparents while Justin ran to the phone shack and called an ambulance."

"How long ago was this?"

"A little over an hour ago, maybe closer to two."

So Abe had been riding in an ambulance as they had been eating pie and laughing about the day. Olivia Mae looked up and met Noah's gaze, and he knew she was thinking the same thing.

"Can I—can I see him?"

"I'm sure you can. Let me go and tell the nurse that you're here—and that you're next of kin." Lucas winked, which did more to ease Noah's worries than anything he'd said. If Abe was in any sort of danger, Lucas would be somber and proper. The fact that he was kidding around was a good thing.

As Lucas walked away, Sarah and Justin made it over to where they were waiting.

"I'm sorry, Olivia Mae. I thought I was watching closely, but..."

Instead of answering right away Olivia Mae stood and put her arms around Sarah. They hugged and cried and finally pulled apart when Justin suggested they might need some fresh air.

"You two are acting *narrisch*. Lucas said Abe's going to be all right. What's all the tears for?"

"Men," Olivia Mae said.

"We're *gut*," Sarah said. "I am so sorry..."

"Don't mention it again. He could have fallen

anytime." Olivia Mae wiped at her tears, the first that she'd allowed to fall since receiving the news about her *daddi*. "It could have happened while I was there. It's just…he's a little wobbly at times."

Noah saw Lucas trying to catch their attention. He touched Olivia Mae's shoulder and nodded toward where their bishop was waiting, motioning for her to join him.

"I'll be praying, and I'll wait right here."

"Danki."

And then she was gone, disappearing through the double doors and down the hall.

Olivia Mae walked beside Lucas, her heart hammering in her chest. She trusted what he said. She believed that *Daddi* was going to be okay, but she needed to see him for herself. She needed to see with her own eyes that he was fine.

And what about *Mammi*? How was she handling the emergency?

When they made it to the room with the name *Abe Lapp* scrawled on the whiteboard beside the door, they paused outside the doorway. Lucas touched her arm, then turned and silently made his way back down the hall. Olivia Mae stood there, studying her grandparents through the small window. Fear and relief and joy and sorrow coursed through her veins all at the same moment. So many thoughts and feelings collided within her that for a few seconds the hall began to spin and she had to reach for the door frame.

She closed her eyes, swallowed twice, prayed for the peace that passes all understanding.

When she opened her eyes again, she pushed her nose right up to the glass—still not ready to enter, still needing to see.

Daddi had his head bandaged, but his eyes were closed and his color was good. She could tell by the numbers on the digital screen that his blood pressure and heart rate were both in acceptable ranges. She'd been through this before—several times now. She'd learned her way around a hospital.

It was the image of *Mammi* that she thought she'd never forget. Sitting beside *Daddi*, her back was to the door, her head bowed, her hand covering his. Olivia Mae knew without a shadow of a doubt that her grandmother was praying—for his health, his recovery, their time together, even for Olivia Mae.

She knew her grandmother's heart like she knew her own.

They were that close to one another.

They shared the same fears and hopes and memories.

And suddenly standing in that hospital doorway, Olivia Mae felt a shower of gratitude cascade over her. She understood that she'd been given a great gift once again—the gift of another evening with the people she loved. She bowed her head and thanked the Lord that He had once again seen fit to keep *Daddi* here with them a little longer, that they had so many friends waiting back in the little room down the hall, that Sarah and Justin and Noah were a part of her life.

But the prayer of thanksgiving clashed with another—as her heart cried out to God to see her through the next few weeks and months. Because she knew, without a doubt now, that they would be moving to Maine. She couldn't handle this alone anymore. She'd been a fool to try. And anything she felt for Noah? Well, it would have to wait.

Pulling back her shoulders and breathing deeply, she pushed the door open and stepped into the room. *Mammi* glanced back over her shoulder. Her expression broke into a smile and she stood. "*Gut*, you found us."

"Of course I found you, *Mammi*." The tears came fully then. The tears that she'd been holding back streamed down her cheeks. "I was so scared, when Justin told us—"

Mammi had stood and wobbled over to where

Olivia Mae was waiting. "He's fine. Your *daddi* is fine."

"I should have been home."

"You know that isn't true."

Mammi placed her hands—hands that were as soft as a newborn's skin, though wrinkled and spotted and frail—on both sides of Olivia Mae's face. Olivia Mae closed her eyes for a moment and willed herself to remember this feeling, this love that was so precious.

"It could have happened while you were there. Abe could have fallen anytime and anywhere." *Mammi* hugged her, then returned to *Daddi*'s side to check him again and pull the covers up a bit. "We're old is all. Old age isn't something to be avoided at all costs, Olivia Mae. But it does have its challenges."

Instead of sitting back down, she motioned Olivia Mae toward the chair and whispered, "I think I'll step down the hall—say hello to folks and let them know that Abe is going to be fine."

Olivia Mae took her place and did the same thing that she'd been watching her *mammi* do— she prayed. For her grandfather, for the doctors, for her brothers and even for the people who would purchase their little farm. She prayed for the new home waiting for them in Maine. She prayed for herself and for Noah.

It was while she was sitting there, alone in

the hospital room, watching the monitor's numbers flash on the small screen and the IV fluid drip into the tube that led to his arm, that *Daddi* opened his eyes.

He didn't seem to notice where he was or that there was an IV attached to his arm. He certainly didn't seem in pain, though that may have been because of some medication they gave him. Instead he simply smiled at her, reached for her hand and said, "Olivia Mae, it's *gut* to see you."

"Ya?" She once again found herself blinking back tears. How long had it been since he'd called her by her name? Why now, tonight of all nights, was he lucid?

Perhaps because she needed him to be.

Maybe because he was relaxed from the medication or the brief rest.

Or possibly this was one of those moments of grace that *Gotte* sent to calm her soul.

It was several hours later before she walked back out into the waiting room and headed toward the front of the hospital. Her *mammi* had sent everyone home, insisting they get some rest and come to see Abe when he was released from the hospital.

Everyone had done as she'd suggested—everyone except for Noah. He jumped to his feet and waited, his eyes searching hers. He didn't pepper her with questions. He didn't rush her. He simply waited.

She stopped in the middle of the room, her eyes taking in the empty chairs and then coming back to rest on him, her heart understanding that he had waited for her. She felt strong now and unafraid, and still she walked straight into his arms.

He let her rest there, and when she finally pulled away, he asked, "Are you okay?"

"Ya."

"Abe?"

"Resting, and they brought *Mammi* a blanket and pillow. The chair makes out into a bed. She wouldn't leave him."

"You're going home?"

"She insisted."

"May I take you? Justin and Sarah left me the buggy. Lucas took them home."

"Ya. That would be *gut."*

"I'm a little surprised you're not staying," he said as they walked toward the parking area. "You're nearly as stubborn as Rachel."

"I didn't think she'd rest as long as I was in the room, and there was only the one chair. So I pretended to agree with her. Honestly I'm not sure how I planned to get home, now that I think about it. I'd completely forgotten that I'd ridden here in Justin's buggy. I guess I would have called a cab, if there'd been no other way…"

"Glad I can be of service." Noah opened the door on her side of the buggy and faked a bow. "Welcome to Snickers's limo."

"Fancy."

"*Ya*, I know." He brushed back a lock of hair that had escaped from her *kapp* and kissed her softly. "You look exhausted. I'm glad you're going to get some rest."

"Actually I'm going to see to Zeus and the sheep."

"I would have done that."

"I know you would have." She squeezed his hand and then climbed up into the buggy.

"Sarah feels terrible about what happened."

"Nothing about tonight was her fault, and this isn't the first time he's fallen. That's one of the reasons we picked up all of the rugs."

"You're fortunate he didn't break a hip."

"I read once that elderly people don't fall and break a hip. What usually happens is they're standing, the hip breaks and then they fall."

Noah glanced at her in surprise. "I didn't know that. You know a lot about this sort of thing."

"What sort of thing?"

"Caring for your grandparents. You're a *gut* granddaughter."

"I've done my best, but I think—I think my opposition to change caused me to wait a little longer than I should have."

"He could have fallen in Maine, too."

"It's true. I only mean that *Mammi* could use more family around her—more than just me. And there's something else that occurred to me while I was sitting beside his hospital bed."

"What's that?"

"I've been dragging my feet—not wanting to move, not wanting to upset their daily routine. And I think I had good reasons for doing that."

"You love them."

"I do, and I'm concerned—always concerned for them." Olivia Mae stared out at the streets of Goshen as they drove toward the farm. The clip-clop of Snickers's hooves on the pavement soothed her nerves, and the night air felt good after being cooped up inside the hospital. She glanced back at Noah, who was still waiting patiently for her to finish her line of thought.

"At the same time I think that putting off moving them was a bit selfish of me. My *bruders* and their wives, my nieces and nephews, they deserve a chance to spend time with *Mammi* and *Daddi*. These final years—they're precious."

Instead of answering, Noah reached across the seat and covered her hand with his.

"If you don't mind, I'd like to stop by the phone shack."

"Call your *bruders*?"

"I'll leave a message. They need to know."

What was left unsaid between them was that most likely this would escalate the efforts to sell *Daddi*'s farm. And what did that mean for their relationship, their growing feelings for one another?

They traveled in silence, the gentle sway of the buggy nearly lulling Olivia Mae to sleep. The next thing she knew, Noah was standing outside of her open door, touching her arm. He said, "We're here. At the phone shack."

She nodded, rubbed her eyes and stumbled into the small building. She'd forgotten her purse, but Noah fetched the required change out of his pocket and dropped it into the coffee can on the counter.

She left her message—rambling a bit but managing to convey the basic facts.

Daddi had fallen.

He was in the hospital.

Both he and *Mammi* were fine.

She'd call the following evening, at six if possible, and give them an update.

When she walked back out of the phone shack, Noah was sitting on the steps. Though she knew she needed to get home, though every muscle in her body was suddenly exhausted and screaming for sleep, she sat beside him, her head on his shoulder, and together they watched the stars come out.

The next three weeks flew by. *Daddi* came home after just two days and much of their life returned to normal. It was Olivia Mae who had changed. She finally understood and accepted that they would be moving—and sooner than later if her brother had anything to say about it.

She continued to see Noah at church functions, and he stopped by the house at least twice a week to check on them. But she felt herself pulling back. Why lose more of her heart to this dear man who had become so important to her?

She couldn't make their future come together in her head.

They would be moving to Maine.

Noah had an excellent job here in Indiana—not to mention all of his family was here.

She couldn't see it working, so instead she focused on preparing for the move. Her biggest concern was what she'd do with her sheep, but Noah told her not to worry.

"That's like telling a mother not to worry about her children."

"Oh, they're children now, are they?" He could always make her laugh and never failed to point out the lighter side of things exactly when she needed to be reminded that all was not somber and gray. "What do you call a sheep covered in chocolate?"

Olivia Mae pretended to groan.

"A candy ba-a-a-aaa." Satisfied that he'd at least made her smile, Noah grew suddenly serious. "I'll take care of the sheep, Olivia Mae. If that's what you're worried about, if you're sure that you're going to move—"

"What choice do I have?"

"If that's the way you feel, then I will take care of the sheep."

"You don't know anything about sheep, and I know you don't want to be a farmer."

"I could auction them."

She must have looked horrified because he quickly added, "I'm kidding. I'll learn. I don't mind learning—for you."

She would miss him terribly when they moved. She realized now what a precious thing friendship was. And love? Well, love was a blessing from *Gotte*, plain and simple. Each time she saw Noah, she pushed aside her fears and worries and tried to enjoy the minutes they had together.

And then, one month later, when a string of rainy days was broken by bright afternoon sunshine, she walked to the phone shack and saw the recorder blinking with the number 1. She knew then, before she even pressed Play, that it was her brother. They'd found a buyer. Someone who wanted to expedite the process. It was time for her to begin to pack.

That evening, she broke the news to Noah.

Chapter Thirteen

He drove around for more than an hour—not ready to go home, not sure exactly when he'd lost his heart to Olivia Mae Miller. But the fact remained that he had, and now it was time to step up and decide what to do about it.

He unharnessed the horse and tossed some feed into a bucket. He might have gone to his room and tossed and turned all night, but when he walked into the kitchen he was surprised to see his *mamm* there, her hands wrapped around a steaming cup of what he knew was herbal tea. On the table was a plate of peanut-butter squares that she pushed toward him. "Cold milk in the fridge," she said.

He poured a glass and made his way through two of the squares before he found his voice.

"She's leaving earlier than I thought."

"To Maine?"

"*Ya.* Her *bruder* has already found a buyer for the place. He'll be here to move them next week."

She didn't say anything, didn't offer an opinion or a suggestion, simply waited for him to work through his thoughts and emotions.

Finally, he sighed and pushed the plate of sweets away. "I love her."

"And that's bad?"

"This situation—*our* situation—is problematic."

"How so?"

He sat back and studied her. His mom had always been the listener of the family, perhaps because she was the only female. Growing up, it had helped tremendously for him to know that he could trust her, that he could share with her the things that were bothering him. When he'd become a teenager, he'd suddenly grown shy about that, and perhaps that was when his problems had started—when he'd stopped sharing his hurts and fears and dreams with the people who loved him. So instead of shrugging, and offering a noncommittal response, he stared up at the ceiling and tried to articulate what was standing between him and the love of his life.

"Her family situation with her grandparents is difficult."

"Because of their health."

"And because she feels responsible for them, in the way a parent is for a child." He held out his hand, palm up, then turned it palm down. "Things have reversed."

"Not an easy situation."

"But that isn't the worst of it."

His *mamm* crossed her arms on the table and leaned forward.

"The worst of it is that I want what's best for her, what's best for Olivia Mae, and I don't know what that is. Is it moving to Maine? Starting over? Having help with Abe and Rachel? Or is it staying here? Do I even have a right to ask that of her?"

"It's a *gut* thing that you realize you love her now, before she leaves."

"Is it? Because at the moment it only feels miserable."

She patted his hand, picked up his glass and her mug and rinsed them in the sink. By the time she returned to the table he was sitting there with his head in his hands.

Her next words surprised him because they weren't about love or marriage or families—things that he knew she held dear. Instead she said, "I'm proud of you, Noah. You've turned into a fine young man."

"I'm twenty-nine, *Mamm*. I've been a man for a long time now."

"In some ways, I suppose that's true." She sat next to him and waited for him to raise his eyes to hers. "But in other ways it's happened in these last few weeks. When you learn to put others' needs first, over your own. When even in the midst of your own dreams and desires, your heart is set on easing the way for the person you love. Well, that's the difference between a boy and a man."

She stood, kissed him on top of the head, as she'd done for all of his life, and walked out of the kitchen.

He was left with her words echoing through his mind.

He supposed what she'd said was true, because he no longer felt like a *youngie*. He felt as if his heart were breaking in two, but that seemed almost minor compared to what Olivia Mae was facing. The thing that twisted his stomach into a knot was admitting that he didn't know what was best for her. How could he know? Those decisions were hers to make.

One thing he knew for sure—he wouldn't make the mistake of waiting to find out. His only regret would be not asking her what she wanted for her future.

If it was staying in Goshen, he would find a way to make that happen.

If it was going to Maine, then he'd help in any way he could to make that transition smooth.

And if she wanted him in her life, then he would give up anything because sacrificing something for Olivia Mae wasn't really a sacrifice at all.

Her happiness was what mattered the most to him. Olivia Mae was a *gut* person. She deserved her own family and her own home, but she also felt a strong responsibility to her grandparents. She wasn't a young girl, but a woman with all the emotions and needs and responsibilities of a woman.

And he loved her beyond anything he could imagine.

He took off his shoes and crept upstairs to his room, trying not to wake anyone. He needn't have worried. Justin was walking out of the bathroom, drying his hair with a towel.

"Sarah asleep?"

"Nearly. The baby was kicking a lot this afternoon so she didn't get a nap."

Noah nodded toward his bedroom. He turned on the lantern, and his brother sat on his bed while he took the chair.

"I have one week."

"What do you mean?"

"I mean I have one week…to convince Olivia Mae that we're meant for each other."

Justin had continued drying his hair with the towel, but now he let it drop around his neck. "I thought you had a month."

"So did I." Noah picked up a pen from the desk and twirled it in his fingers.

"What happened?"

"Her *bruder* called this afternoon. Told her he'd found a buyer for the house, and that he'd be down in one week to move them."

"Wow."

"Uh-huh."

"So what's your plan?"

"I don't have one. That's why I'm talking to you."

Instead of answering, Justin finished drying his hair, stood and returned the towel to the bathroom. Walking back into Noah's room, he asked, "So are you sure?"

"Sure about what?"

"That you love her?"

"*Ya.* I don't know when it happened. Maybe when I was sitting on her porch having our first lesson. Maybe when I walked into her house and saw the roof leaking like a sieve. Or maybe that first day when I gave her the letter box."

"This isn't you wanting to rescue her, is it? Because I don't think that's the same thing as love."

"She's the one who rescued me." It came out

more of a growl than he intended, the admission piercing his heart but also firming his resolve.

They both turned toward the open window as an owl hooted from a nearby tree. The storms of the recent days had passed, leaving the evening cool and pleasant.

"You're going to need a plan."

"Like what?"

"I don't know. What did you learn in those lessons she was giving you?"

They sat there for another half hour, as Noah explained the things he'd learned about dating, women and how to relate to someone else. By the time they were done, Noah understood that he'd learned about more than romantic relationships. He'd learned how to connect to people in general. While he might always be an introvert, be more comfortable around a few people than a crowd of them, he no longer had to avoid someone that he could care about.

And with that knowledge came the certainty of what he needed to do next.

When his brother left for his own room, Noah turned the lantern up to its brightest setting. The small desk in the corner of his room was well-stocked. His *mamm* must have been using it when he'd lived away, because he'd never needed pen, paper and envelopes. Now all that he needed was there—another example of *Gotte*'s provision. He pulled out a clean sheet of paper and began writing a note.

It took him three tries to get it right—to put his hopes and dreams on that sheet of paper without scaring off Olivia Mae. He understood that she was afraid of putting her heart on the line. She was also strong and kind and wise beyond her years. But change, especially big change, was always frightening.

So his first goal was to calm that fear.

His second was to pique her interest.

And his third? Well, his third was to win her heart. Which was expecting a lot from a one-page note.

After he'd done his best, he folded it neatly, stuck it into an envelope and scrawled her name across it.

Olivia Mae Miller.

If things went as he hoped and prayed they would, that would change. Personally he thought Olivia Mae Graber had a much nicer ring to it.

Olivia Mae hurried in from the barn as the sun was popping over the horizon. She hoped she hadn't made her grandparents wait too late to eat. She'd told them time and time again to start without her, but they never would.

Mammi was placing an egg casserole on the table and looked up to smile as Olivia Mae paused at the mudroom door to knock any dirt off her shoes. As she walked to the sink to wash her hands, she stole a glance at the table. Her *mammi* was following the nurse's instructions to a *T*. A bowl of fruit and a platter of hot biscuits sat in the middle of the table—along with butter and jars of peach, apple and strawberry preserves. Olivia Mae said good morning, poured herself a cup of coffee and plopped into her seat, which was when she noticed the envelope with her name on it. How could she not notice it? The envelope was positioned across the middle of her plate.

"What's this?"

"Looks like a letter."

"*Ya*, but—"

"Noah brought it by earlier."

"Noah Graber?"

"Don't know any other Noah." *Mammi*'s eyes twinkled as she sat down across from her.

"Earlier this morning?" She glanced up at the clock. It was only a few minutes past six thirty, and she hadn't heard a buggy. Then again, she'd been in the back of the barn mucking out stalls.

"We invited that nice young man to stay to eat, but he said he had to get to work." *Daddi* reached for a biscuit and broke it open, releasing steam and a scrumptious yeasty scent. "Do we know him?"

"*Ya*, for sure and certain we do. Let me put some butter on the biscuit for you, Abe."

Olivia Mae couldn't imagine why Noah would drop off a letter for her before going to work. That meant he'd harnessed the horse to the buggy, driven to their house, dropped off the letter, and driven back home in time to unharness the horse and catch the shuttle to the auction in Shipshewana.

"This came while I was in the barn?"

"It did." *Mammi* scooped a helping of eggs onto *Daddi*'s plate and then another onto hers. She pushed the casserole dish toward Olivia Mae, who shook her head. She was still holding the envelope as if she was afraid to open it.

Why would Noah Graber write her a letter?

What was he up to?

And why was her heart galloping like a mare set free in the pasture?

She had precious little time to get ready for the move and a long list of things to do today. She did not have the luxury of pining over what might or might not be in a mysterious envelope. Gulping down half her mug of coffee for courage, she stuck her fingernail under the envelope's seal and ripped it open.

Dear Olivia Mae,
I would like to ask for the pleasure of your

company this evening at 6:00 p.m. for a picnic dinner. I realize you are quite busy this week packing the house, but everyone needs to eat. More important, we have only a few days left until your move, and spending what time we have together is important to me.

Of course, I will bring all of the necessary supplies. You only need to be on your front porch at 6:00 p.m. And before you say you need to eat with your grandparents—remember you will have all of the weeks and months stretching out into the future to spend with them. Our time is slipping away.

We won't be gone more than a couple hours, but if you'd like a sitter for your grandparents, I can arrange that. And I promise to have you home by nine so you won't be too tired tomorrow.

If you're agreeable to this, call the phone shack near my house and leave a message. However, if you feel you can't get away, there's no need to take the time to go all the way to the phone shack. I understand how busy you are, especially as you prepare for your journey to Maine.

Sincerely yours,

Noah

She read it once and then again. The first time through she was sure that she must refuse him. The second time through she wondered if she dared to take a few hours for herself. But when she raised her eyes and looked at *Mammi* and *Daddi*, who were both smiling at her, she knew what her answer would be.

Pushing back her chair, she said, "I'm going to ride my bike down to the phone shack. I won't be long."

As she pedaled down the lane, the letter tucked in her apron pocket, the tension that had been building since her brother's phone call melted away.

While it was true that her life was changing, the sun was still shining brightly, there was a pleasant breeze, and she felt young and healthy.

Did Noah Graber want to court her?

Did she want to be courted by him? She poked at the feelings that she had for Noah, like one might poke at a toothache. It was true that he was handsome, nice to be around and a *gut* person, but nothing in the letter suggested he felt as she did. He hadn't even tried to kiss her again in the last week.

Noah was a *gut* friend; that was the reason for the dinner invitation.

Or was there something more going on?

Did Noah care for her?

Was he actually asking her out on a date now that she was moving? His timing was terrible! But his letter was spot-on.

He'd appreciated what a stressful time this was.

He'd given her an easy out if she wanted to decline.

He'd respected her time, and he'd understood her need for a break from her grandparents.

Noah had come a long way from the clueless guy who thought he was happy being a bachelor. The night before she'd made a list of possible women he could date, wanting to fulfill her promise to give him three solid chances and wanting to do so before they moved. But each name she'd listed, she'd crossed out.

Oh, they were nice girls, but for some reason each one had seemed wrong for Noah.

So who was the right woman for him?

Why did the thought of matching him with someone else cause her heart to sink?

She let that question roll around while she parked her bike, hurried into the phone shack and left her message, which was short and sweet. "This message is for Noah Graber, and my answer is yes. Yes, I'd love to."

She stepped out of the phone shack into a summer morning that was as close to perfect as any she'd ever seen.

The sky was blue, the day promised to be warm and a light breeze stirred the trees.

And she was going on a date with Noah Graber.

How long had it been since she'd stepped out with a boy, since she'd done something for herself? For years now her very existence had been focused on two things—caring for her grandparents and matching others to their true love. Suddenly that seemed short-sighted. In fact, it seemed as if she'd neglected something very important.

She'd turned her back on her own hopes and dreams.

It was all good and fine to care about your family, but Olivia Mae wasn't one to encourage being a martyr. *Gotte* had a plan for every life, and it was possible—yes, it was actually certain—that He had a plan for hers. The question was, did it include Noah Graber?

The day passed quickly. Jane and Francine arrived with packing boxes and insisted on staying until lunch, helping her pack dishes, linens and clothes they wouldn't be needing in the next week. Everything was carefully labeled and then carried to the barn and stored. She didn't want the boxes in the house, where

Mammi might trip over them and *Daddi* continually asked, "Is someone moving?"

It was when they were taking a break on the front porch, each holding a cold glass of tea and a snack, that Jane broached the subject of dating. "I've stepped out three evenings now with Elijah."

It was the first time she'd brought Elijah up in front of Olivia Mae, who asked, "How did that go?"

"*Gut.* He…he's enjoying working at the factory, or at least enjoying the pay."

They all three laughed about that. It was common knowledge that the factory paid well.

"More important, he's learning to use the modern equipment for the woodworking. Elijah says what he really wants to do is start his own business specializing in custom-built cabinets, that sort of thing. He knows that some of the modern tools wouldn't be allowed, but others would—many are now powered by batteries, which he could charge with a generator in the barn if the bishop allows it."

"I can see him being *gut* at that." Francine bit into the apple she'd chosen over a cookie. The tea—of course—was unsweetened.

"Do you have feelings for him?" Olivia Mae asked.

"*Ya.* I do." Jane wiped the condensation off

her glass and rubbed it on the back of her neck. "Now that I understand him better, I realize that he has a real talent for working with wood. He never would have been happy as a farrier. I don't know why I couldn't see that before. Somehow, I took his rejection of his *dat*'s plans for his life as a rejection of me. Now I know he was just trying to find himself."

"Aren't we all," Francine murmured.

Olivia Mae almost let her comment slide, but she had six days left in town and while they would continue to write letters to one another, writing wasn't the same as speaking face-to-face.

"What do you mean by that, Francine?"

"Oh." Her gaze jerked up, as if she didn't realize she'd spoken aloud. "I guess while we're confessing, I might as well do the same."

"I thought we were just talking." Jane's grin widened. "But I like confessions, too."

Francine sat up straighter. "I've applied for a position with MDS."

"Mennonite Disaster Services?" Olivia Mae leaned forward and squeezed Francine's hand. "That's *wunderbaar*."

"It's fantastic," Jane agreed.

"Do you think so? Because I haven't told my *bruder* yet or my parents. But I think—I think I'll like it. They do important work for people affected by disasters. And they need a cook for a crew in Texas, where they're still helping folks with hurricane recovery. It would be a three-month job, but possibly renewable for as long as they're in the area."

"You're a very *gut* cook."

"It doesn't pay, but they provide lodging and meals are free. More important, I think it would give me time away from Goshen, which is what I feel like I need right now."

"They would be fortunate to have you," Olivia Mae said.

"The question is whether they'll approve me, because of my diabetes."

"I don't think you have to worry about that, and it's because of your diabetes that you know so much about nutrition." Olivia Mae set her rocker into motion. The two women in front of her had become more than friends—they were like sisters—and she realized in that moment how much she would miss them.

"Why are you smiling?" Jane asked.

"She looks like she knows something we don't."

"Looks like she wants to share a secret."

"And now she's blushing."

"Okay, you can stop. It's not that big a deal, only that... Well, Noah asked me out for dinner tonight." When she told them it was for a picnic, they all three burst into laughter. It did Olivia Mae's heart good to see that Francine could laugh about Noah's ill-conceived date and the argument that had ensued. Both seemed like they'd happened long ago rather than earlier that summer.

"Just watch out for the horse blanket," Francine said, draining her glass and then standing. "Now let's get back to packing so you have time to prepare for your date."

Olivia Mae had used that phrase so often in her role as matchmaker—*prepare for your date*—as if it was a recipe that needed to have all the ingredients set out on the counter. But in truth she had been ready for tonight since the first day Noah had stepped on her grandparents' porch. She had no idea where the evening would lead, or if she was making too big a deal of it, but she knew with a deep certainty that it felt good to look forward to something for a change.

Noah arrived at Olivia Mae's place a few minutes early. Instead of turning into the lane, he pulled to the side of the road and waited. Arriving early would only make her feel rushed, and that was the last thing he wanted to do.

When his watch said five minutes before six, he called out to Snickers, who tossed her head and then trotted down the lane. It was almost as if the horse understood this was an important evening, or perhaps she was picking up on Noah's enthusiasm.

He thought he was ready for just about anything, but then he drew close to the porch and saw Olivia Mae standing there. She wore her light gray dress, clean white apron and a shawl the color of the summer sky across her shoulders. Noah's heart felt as if it stopped beating completely, then stammered and then galloped forward. He raised a hand to wave, murmured to the horse and jumped out of the buggy.

"Noah."

"Olivia Mae."

"Beautiful evening."

"Ya." It was as if the thoughts in his head had decided to shut down, but then he remembered sitting on the porch with her as she explained that women were more like men than different from them. Women liked to be appreciated, cared for, admired—same as anyone. So he stepped closer and said, "You look *wunderbaar.* That shawl, it's a nice color."

"This?" A smile tugged at the corners of her mouth.

"Did you buy it in town?"

"I made it."

Now her smile had broadened and any anxiety he felt slipped away. This was Olivia Mae, his friend, and the woman he hoped to marry. He didn't have to worry about being someone he wasn't. He only had to find the time and place to share his feelings.

"I'd like to say hello to your grandparents before we leave."

"Of course." Her voice had dropped to a whisper, and he thought her eyes looked bright with unshed tears. Before he could think that through, she'd turned and led him into the living room.

"Where are the packing boxes?" he whispered.

"Stacked in the barn. Bothers *Daddi* less that way."

"Evening, Abe."

The old man looked up in surprise. He'd been shelling peas, but he stopped, cocked his head and said, "Do I know you?"

"*Ya*, I'm Noah. Noah Graber."

"I knew some Grabers once. They own a farm closer to town."

"That would be my parents." They'd had this conversation before, several times, but Noah understood that the present often slipped away from Abe while the past anchored him to a safe place. "My *dat* helped you to build the barn. I was a young lad then, but I remember us all meeting early on a Saturday morning."

"And finishing it by evening." A look of contentment spread over Abe's face as he returned his attention to the peas. "We appreciate that. The barn, it's going to be a real help for our first winter here."

"*Ya*, I suspect it will."

Noah met Olivia Mae's gaze and she mouthed a silent *danki*.

Rachel walked into the room, carrying two steaming mugs. "Noah, I didn't hear your buggy."

"Let me carry those for you." He was across the room in three steps, taking the mugs and carrying them to the small table between the two rockers.

"We're just settling down for a little snack. Abe, he likes to go to bed early."

As if in agreement, Abe yawned, but he continued shelling the peas.

"Is there anything I can do to help this week?" He meant with the move, but he didn't want to upset Abe by mentioning it. "Anything you need?"

"The best things are not things." Rachel smiled at the old proverb. "If there is, I'll let you know. Now go, both of you. It's a beautiful summer evening. You don't need to spend it inside with two old people."

Noah reached for Olivia Mae's hand. Entwining his fingers with hers, he led her out to the buggy, helped her climb up into the seat and then hurried around to the other side.

The best things are not things.

How true that was. He'd thought that his life goal was to be an auctioneer, to have his own bachelor pad, to be free of others' expectations. But those things paled in comparison to the woman sitting beside him.

They spoke of the weather, Jane, Francine and general happenings within their community. He let Olivia Mae drive the conversation and when they fell into a comfortable silence, he enjoyed it rather than worrying what it might mean. When they were a mile away from his brother's place, he started to laugh.

"Care to share?" She adjusted herself in the buggy, waiting, one eyebrow raised and a smile on her face.

"I was just remembering my first date, with Jane. Did I ever tell you that I penned talking points on the inside of my hand? Thought I should have them there in case I couldn't think of anything to say."

"Oh, my."

"Uh-huh, and as she said, I barely let her get a word in edgewise. Silence—especially silence when I was with a woman—sort of scared me."

"And now?"

"Now silence feels comfortable, like we're sharing something without the need to put it into words."

Her cheeks blossomed pink, and he had to fight the urge to pull the buggy over on the side of the road and kiss her. Instead he turned his attention to the mare, intent on not missing the turn into his brother's back pasture.

"Where are we going?"

"Private little place I heard about."

"Heard about?"

"Okay. It's my *bruder*'s place—Samuel's. There's a nice pond near the back, with shade trees around it."

"Is that so?"

"And I have the owner's word that we'll have the place all to ourselves."

He pulled into the back entrance of the property, called out to Snickers to *whoa* and hopped down to open the gate. When he'd pulled through, Olivia Mae offered to close the gate, but he shook his head and took care of it quickly. The lane was a little bumpy, but the horse seemed happy to be on a less-traveled road.

When they pulled up to the pond, he knew that his brother had picked the perfect spot. Justin claimed he took Sarah there for all their important occasions—when he'd first kissed her, when he'd proposed—and she'd taken him there when she told him about the baby. It was quiet and private and peaceful. Perhaps the area would become a sort of living testament to their families and their love for one another. That thought cheered him immensely and calmed the nerves in his stomach.

The pond was full due to recent rains, large trees shaded the east and south side, and a small dock reached out a good ten feet into the water.

After setting the brake on the buggy and tying Snickers's lead to a metal rail his brother had installed for just that purpose, he helped Olivia Mae out of the buggy. Reaching into the back seat, he snagged the picnic basket and quilt.

"Can I help you carry that?"

"*Nein*. I've got it." He didn't let go of her hand as they walked to the far side of the pond. Though his heart was pounding in his chest he felt good—better than he'd felt in a very long time. He didn't know what turns their relationship might take over the next few hours, but he knew that he was where he wanted to be at this moment, and he planned on enjoying that instead of worrying.

He'd done enough worrying the night before to last him a lifetime. Now that he was with Olivia Mae, he knew that whatever happened would be what *Gotte* intended. But he certainly hoped that he and the man upstairs were seeing eye to eye.

Chapter Fourteen

Olivia Mae ran her fingers over the old quilt as Noah pulled food from the basket. The design was a double wedding-ring pattern. Had he chosen it on purpose? Did he understand the symbolism of the quilt? Though Amish didn't exchange rings, the idea of interlocking circles, intertwined lives, was one they could appreciate.

She glanced at him and caught him watching her.

"I brought salad." He held up a container. "I remembered you saying how every meal needs one."

"You were listening."

"I was. Also have some sliced ham and turkey—wasn't sure which you'd want—along with cheddar and Swiss cheese, fresh bread and all the other stuff you put on a sandwich."

"A well-planned meal," she teased.

"Which isn't complete without dessert." He held up a container of cookies. "Chocolate pecan. Your favorite, right?"

She lunged for the cookies, but he jerked them away at the last second and held them over his head. Then they were laughing and acting like two teenagers. His hand on hers caused goose bumps to dot her arms. She thought he was about to kiss her, their faces so close she could smell spearmint on his breath. Instead he pressed his forehead to hers and said, *"Danki."*

"For what?"

He pulled back and studied her a minute, as if he was weighing his answer. Finally he said simply, "Agreeing to come to dinner with me."

"I should be thanking you. This is a *wunder-baar* meal you've put together, and you were right—it does help to take a few hours away from the packing."

She began to relax as they put together two sandwiches that looked cartoonish in their height. He'd packed silverware for the potato salad, cloth napkins, bottles of water and cans of pop, as well as a thermos of coffee.

"Don't know how you fit so much in that basket."

"It's very special."

"The basket?"

"*Ya.* For sure and certain. Bought it from the auction, and thought to myself that this basket would be perfect for a picnic with Olivia Mae."

"So you've been planning this for some time."

"Maybe. In the back of my mind." He took a bite of the sandwich, but held up his hand as if he had more to say. When he'd finished chewing and taken a long pull from a bottle of water, he added, "Truthfully, it threw me for a loop when you told me your move is in a week."

"*Ya.* I felt the same way. I still do."

"I've been trying to gather my courage to do this, to take you on a real date and not an instructional one."

She shook her head, trying not to laugh. "That first lesson, on my porch..."

"Rainstorm nearly blew the table over. And you weren't going to let me inside."

"I was embarrassed." She stared out over the pond. "And proud. I suppose that was part of my problem."

"Didn't know a roof could leak that much and still hold together."

"The look on your face when you walked inside." She dared glance at him now and was relieved to see that he found the memory as funny as she did.

"Roofs are easy to fix. I know the situation with your grandparents is more complicated."

"It is."

"As far as overcoming my shyness and *learning I can be comfortable in someone else's presence…*"

"I shouldn't have suggested otherwise."

"*Nein.* It was true. I'd never thought of it that way. I always told myself there was no point because it wouldn't end well."

"Sometimes that's easier than trying."

"Agreed." He took another bite from the sandwich, then a few moments later added, "But knowing that our time is limited, that spurred me to action."

Olivia Mae didn't answer right away. She had so many thoughts spinning around in her mind that she didn't know which to say first, so she gave herself a minute. She couldn't believe that she—Olivia Mae Miller, Matchmaker Extraordinaire—felt so completely off-kilter by a simple date. It was one thing to teach something to someone, to advise others, but it was another thing entirely to experience it herself. She'd forgotten so much.

The heightened emotions.

The way that every minor touch felt like a jolt of electricity.

The anticipation and dread that mingled together.

"I'm glad I came tonight."

"Ya?"

She echoed his earlier sentiment. *"Danki."*

"For?"

"Inviting me. Being thoughtful. Knowing what would help. Take your pick."

He cocked his head and seemed about to answer, but instead he shook his head and took another sip of the water he'd opened. They finished the meal watching the birds swoop down over the pond, then a doe and fawn appeared at the far side of the water.

The fawn was only a few weeks old by the look of its wobbly legs. It hid on the far side of the doe, trying to nurse as she drank from the pond. It was covered with spots and occasionally it would stick its head out from behind the doe—all ears and eyes, spots and knobby legs. Olivia Mae thought it might be the most beautiful thing she'd ever seen.

One last drink from the pond and then the mom walked away, though not so quickly that the fawn couldn't follow.

She glanced up to see Noah watching her. "I've seen hundreds of does, but I've never watched one from across a pond as the sun set."

"We're making special memories, *ya*?"

"I suppose we are."

"Care to go for a walk?"

"A walk would be *gut*."

They stored everything back into the hamper except for the container of cookies and thermos of coffee. Then Noah pulled her to her feet, but he didn't release her hand. Instead he again laced his fingers with hers and she marveled at the warmth of that gesture, how it seemed to anchor her world.

Could a small touch do such a big thing?

They walked around the pond, stopping at the dock and then walking out on the wooden planks. The setting sun was sending color across the sky, though they still had probably an hour before darkness settled. The summer evenings in Indiana took their leave gently and slowly.

"Have I ever told you how nervous I was the first day I met you?"

"When you brought me the letter box?"

He nodded as they both sat on the edge of the dock. Olivia Mae pulled off her sandals. Noah laughed as he unlaced his shoes. They could just dip their toes in the water if they stretched.

"I knew you were nervous. You kept twirling that hat."

"If I close my eyes I can still see you standing there. At first I'm pretty sure you just wanted to send me away, and then you saw the box. You stepped out onto the porch and…"

He ducked his head, but still she didn't interrupt. He raised his eyes to meet hers. "You looked like you walked out of a dream. At that moment, all I wanted was to get to know you better."

"I remember you telling me that you were a happy bachelor, and I thought there was no such thing. I might have been wrong about that. Some people...well, I suppose some people are happier alone."

"I'm not one of those people, though. The past weeks with you, they've been the best of my life." He again reached for her hand. "I realize this isn't the best timing with your move and all, and I don't want you to feel pressured. But I need to say it..."

"Say what?"

"That I love you."

Her eyes widened. She hadn't expected this, though she'd known that his feelings for her had grown. The way she cared for him had certainly changed over the past few weeks.

"Olivia Mae, I..."

"Yes?"

"May I ask a question?"

She nodded, unable to talk now, her heart thundering in her chest.

"What are you doing for the rest of your life?" He reached forward, tucked her *kapp* strings behind her shoulders. "When I look at you, I see the girl I'm meant to love for my whole life. I see the woman that I want to eat breakfast with and raise children with and watch sunsets with."

When she didn't answer immediately, he stammered, "I know I won't... I won't always get it right, but I'll try."

She was speechless, utterly dumbfounded. In her wildest dreams she'd thought that perhaps they would begin to court. They'd exchange letters and maybe even visit, though it was a long way from Maine to Indiana. She'd never envisioned a marriage proposal, not on their first date. But it wasn't their first date, not really. And it wasn't sudden. What they felt for each other, it had grown naturally since that Wednesday afternoon when he'd brought her the letter box.

The Noah sitting beside her wasn't the same man who had shown up on her porch. He was confident, or at least hopeful. Even now, he waited patiently for her answer.

"Did you just ask me to marry you?"

"*Ya.* I did." He claimed both of her hands. "We can do this..."

"This?"

"Find our own future, the lives we're meant to live."

She still hadn't answered him. She understood that she needed to say what was in her heart, that now was the time to do that, but the words were frozen in her throat and her hands were shaking and she thought she might be about to have a panic attack.

"Maybe I'm wrong or maybe I'm right, but I had to try."

"You're not wrong."

"Do you love me?"

"*Ya*, Noah. I do." And suddenly the pressure on her heart eased. "I think I've loved you since you walked into my grandparents' house and claimed you were going to fix their roof."

"I've never seen so many pots scattered across the floor."

"And then you followed through—and Noah, it wasn't only that you helped us, but you did it like we were doing you a favor. Like you were happy to help us."

"I was. I *am*."

She looked down at their hands, realizing that she was clutching his as if he was her life preserver in a storm-tossed sea. "And then when you offered to take care of my sheep…"

"I love sheep."

"You're an auctioneer, not a shepherd."

"But I would do it for you."

"I know." The words were a whisper. "And that made all the difference, knowing that you would sacrifice your dream for mine."

"*Nein.*" He rubbed the backs of her hands

with his thumbs. "First, it's not a sacrifice, and second, your dreams are as important to me as mine. We can find a way to have both."

"My grandparents…"

"I don't know the answer, but we'll handle it—together."

He jumped up, helped her to her feet and then stepped closer—close enough that there was only the smallest amount of space between them. He still held her hands, and when he leaned forward, when his lips touched hers, Olivia Mae thought she'd never known such happiness.

They stood there under the final remnants of a glorious sunset, and Olivia Mae stepped into Noah's arms.

The sale of the farm was finalized the week after Noah proposed, but Bishop Lucas was able to find Olivia Mae and her grandparents a place to stay for the rest of the summer. Olivia Mae's brothers came and helped with the move, brought their entire families and promised to return every year. The grandchildren needed to know their grandparents. The *grossdaddi haus* on Widow King's place was small, but there was a pasture for the sheep, and living there gave them the time that they needed.

Noah's *dat* bought a small strip of land across

the road from their family farm. It had been for sale for over a year but, at twenty acres, it was too small to farm. It was, however, perfect for raising a small herd of sheep and pasturing a few horses. A ramshackle house sat on the corner of the property.

Noah and his *bruders* decided it would be quicker and less expensive to pull down the old homestead. They left the foundation and the chimney, then expanded the foundation because a single story would be easier for *Mammi* and *Daddi*. The new home was raised on a Saturday in late August, and a small barn quickly followed.

Daddi continued to have *gut* days and bad days, but he had no problem with the move. *Mammi*'s occasional lapses into the past disappeared completely. Perhaps it had been a way of dealing with stress. Perhaps she'd been more worried about their situation than she'd let on, or maybe as the doctor had suggested it had been a result of the medications that she was taking.

Regardless, both of Olivia Mae's grandparents seemed to have improved by the time they moved into the new home, and they all agreed that living across the street from Noah's parents would be a real help. Olivia Mae hadn't realized how much she'd let her pride stand in the way of accepting help that they desperately needed.

She and Noah were wed on the second Saturday in October.

Jane was there with Elijah. The Sunday before, they'd announced their intention to wed in the spring.

Francine had been accepted for the MDS cook position in Texas, and she was scheduled to leave the following week.

All of Olivia Mae's brothers attended the wedding, as well as all of Noah's family, including his new baby nephew, Silas. Their church family brought the number to nearly two hundred. Looking out over the crowd, she was surprised to see so many couples that she had helped to find one another.

"The matchmaker finally gets matched," Noah whispered.

Olivia Mae wore a forest green dress with a matching apron, and Noah looked so handsome in his new suit that Olivia Mae had trouble taking her eyes off him.

After the singing and sermon, Bishop Lucas called them to the front of the group and they recited their vows, repeating after him and staring into each other's eyes. So much of the day seemed like a blur, like something happening to someone else. Olivia Mae felt as if she was walking through a dream.

Then Lucas presented them as Mr. and Mrs. Noah Graber, and she knew it wasn't a dream. It was her life and her future and her hopes all tossed together into something beautiful— a marriage.

Later that day, as they were about to eat the second meal, Noah tugged at her hand and whispered, "Let's go look at our house."

"But, we're supposed to…"

"Sit at the corner of the table. I know. I promise to have you back before Francine sets down the first plate of chicken casserole."

Instead of going into the house across the road, they walked around to the back, where her sheep were grazing.

"What do you call a dancing sheep?"

"Oh, Noah…" She was standing at the fence, looking at the herd, which would soon grow to nine. When he walked up behind her and put his arms around her, she felt as if she was the happiest woman in the world. She could even forgive him the terrible jokes.

"You know you want to know," he murmured, kissing her cheek.

"Okay. What do you call a dancing sheep?"

"A ba-a-a-llerina."

She covered his hands with hers, wrapping his arms even more tightly around her. "How many of these jokes do you have?"

"Enough to last us a lifetime." He turned her gently so that she was facing him. "I want to say, in case I forget or we get busy with—with living, I want to say that when I saw you standing there this morning, the sunlight shining down on you..." Tears filled his eyes, but he didn't bother to brush them away. "No one ever looked so beautiful."

"Beauty is only skin-deep."

"Not yours." He thumbed away her tears. "Yours goes all the way to the center of your heart. That's what takes my breath away."

"I love you, Noah Graber."

"And I love you, Olivia Mae."

She glanced around at their small farm where they would build their life together, hopefully have children, care for her grandparents and her sheep, and her heart swelled with the joy and hope of their future together.

She and Noah were the perfect match—not because they were the right height for each other or had the same hobbies or even because they felt a very real physical attraction to one another. They were the perfect match because they'd taken the time to truly know one another, and when they did, they'd forged an emotional bond that blossomed into love.

That was *Gotte*'s doing, and Olivia Mae knew in her heart that He was the perfect matchmaker.

* * * * *

If you loved this story,
pick up the other books in the
Indiana Amish Brides series,

A Widow's Hope
Amish Christmas Memories

from bestselling author
Vannetta Chapman

Available now from Love Inspired!

Find more great reads at
www.LoveInspired.com.

Dear Reader,

So often life interrupts our plans. Sometimes we're left feeling like a boat tossed on a stormy sea. During those times, we occasionally bury our dreams believing that they aren't possible, that they'll never happen, that we don't even deserve such happiness.

Olivia Mae has lived just that sort of life. She's compassionate and kind and giving, but in the process she's buried her own dreams. As she cares for her grandparents, she decides that while love and marriage and family aren't things she'll ever experience, she can at least help others on that path. She becomes a matchmaker.

Noah is a confirmed bachelor. He's had relationships in the past that always ended badly. He believes he's defective in some way, and so he envisions a life for himself where he is happy alone. Then he meets Olivia Mae, and they both discover that while they might have given up on their dreams God hasn't. God has a hope and a plan for them. God wants the very best for them, and that best includes all the things they wanted but didn't think they deserved.

I hope you enjoyed reading *A Perfect Amish*

Match. I welcome comments and letters at van-nettachapman@gmail.com.

May we continue "giving thanks always for all things unto God and the Father in the name of our Lord Jesus Christ" (Ephesians 5:20).

Blessings,
Vannetta